CUL DE SAC TALES

Margaret Holbrook

This book is dedicated to
Ste

With love and thanks.

ABOUT THIS BOOK …

Cul De Sac Tales is Margaret Holbrook's second book.

Rita and her neighbours live in a cul de sac. It's the heart of a real community. A community where a certain protocol is followed. It will always be morning coffee, afternoon tea, and definitely not vice versa. But what about … carpet slippers … Cliff Richard cds? … PCSOs?

Why not drop in on the good folk of the cul de sac, and let Rita tell you one or two of their secrets? But there'll be no gossip, they don't tolerate gossip, not in the cul de sac.

A light-hearted look at life in a cul de sac.

THE CUL DE SAC

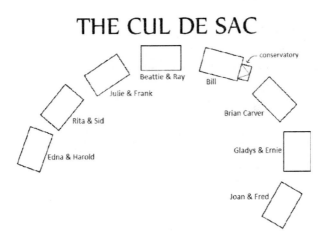

Beattie & Ray

Julie & Frank

Bill

conservatory

Rita & Sid

Brian Carver

Edna & Harold

Gladys & Ernie

Joan & Fred

CONTENTS

Cul De Sac Tales

1 BUNGALOWS, CUL DE SACS, NEIGHBOURS

Hello, I'm Rita. I live in the cul de sac with my husband Sid. I've just been chatting to my neighbours. They've gone in now. I've been in to Sid, I had to wake him, mind. Dozes off at the drop of a hat, he does. Anyway, I just had to tell him...

Our neighbours, Frank and Julie, have been in the house next door for about eighteen months and they have improved the place no end. What Frank couldn't do hadn't been invented. He was a one man whirlwind. I'd spoken to him as you do, being neighbourly and if we were both in the garden, my, could we chat! My husband was a man of few words. I know what you're probably thinking, he couldn't get a word in, but no, you'd be wrong. He was just quiet.

Anyway, to get back to Frank and Julie, their garden was lovely. Frank worked really hard getting everything just so. He'd said he didn't want to let the cul de sac down. He couldn't possibly. We all had to up our game just to keep level with him.

We cul de sac ers are a special breed. It comes of being on a 'no through road'. We only get people who belong. I think you'll agree, if you know anything about anything, that 'cul de sac ers' keep themselves to themselves, as far as mixing with people from 'through roads' goes. On the cul de sac we're just like one big happy family.

When there's a special event, like the Royal Wedding, or the Diamond Jubilee we organise a party. Out come the trestle tables and bunting, (red, white and blue, of course) and we set to and organise. It'll be, 'Are you making the quiche Beattie? 'Good, I'll be sausage rolls and crisps then.' 'Who's doing sandwiches? Joan and Edna,' well, you get the idea. We all muck in and we have a great time.

Anyway where was I? Frank yes, Frank's got a lovely garden and keeps us on our toes. Now did I mention that I'd never spoken to Julie? No, thought I'd forgotten that, well this is it you see, I haven't spoken to her. She nods as they drive off in the car and gives a brief wave from the door when she checks the weather, but I've never spoken to her. Well, that's a lie, I have now, a few moments ago, but I just want to lay down the bones a bit, go over everything so that you can understand where I'm coming from. This is me all over. Sid my husband, says I make things as clear as mud. I hope I'm doing better than that now. Just stop me if I go on too much or veer off the track. That's another thing Sid says I do too much, veer off the track. So just so you know where we're up to, we live in a cul de sac, our neighbours are Frank and Julie. I've a quiet husband, I've spoken to Frank lots and he's a bit of a whizz but I was only on nodding terms with Julie.

Right, so I've also found out they've got grandchildren, George who's ten and Simon two and Ella who'll be four in September. I got all this from Frank. He told me that George will come and stay with them for a month in August, when the school breaks up for the summer. I think he's warning me just in case George is a bit of a tear-away, as youngsters can be sometimes. Oh, that's the other thing, our cul de sac, we're all bungalows. All retired or semi retired. A lot of the ladies volunteer. We work in the local charity shops. It's our way of 'giving back' to our community. Our leader of the cul de sac community group, Bill, says that our cul de sac should be a shining example to the country as a whole. 'We are,' he said, 'shining lights for the prime minister's big society.' We all laughed at this. Bill is a bit of a card really. Always an amusing line or a story to tell but to get back to my story, I was chatting with Frank one day, not long after they'd moved in. Probably about three or four months, something like that and I was singing the praises of bungalow living. How good it was to be on one level, how roomy it was, and how I wouldn't want to move back to a house again, etc, etc. Well, his next remark left me stunned. Notice I say stunned, not shocked. We cul de sac ers are very broadminded. You have to be in this day and age, and after all we are in the 21st century. No, nothing shocks me anymore. I mentioned the whole thing to my husband, Sid. He wasn't shocked either. He didn't say much but I've already told you, he's a man of few words. I can almost hear you thinking, what did Frank say? So, I'll tell you. He said, 'I had a lovely bungalow in Aberystwyth, trouble was I was with the wrong woman.' That was it. No more, no less. Well, as I said I was stunned. I couldn't say very much really. That's another thing, cul de sac ers don't gossip. Not like people who live on through roads. We're a separate breed. 'A breed apart' Sid says, and I believe him. We've been married forty-seven years so I guess after that time you do, believe that is. I'm going off again aren't I? You've not said 'STOP' and I told you to.

So, that's what Frank said. He was in a bungalow in the principality with the wrong woman. I smiled and said I'd got some eggs to whisk, (I was making a Swiss roll) and I left him there in his garden watering the geraniums.

That was it. I never thought any more about it until today. We went on as normal. Sid didn't say much, I chatted with Frank, I'd never chatted to Julie. The reason I spoke to her today, she'd had a colour on her hair. She'd gone from mouse to blonde. Her hair had been cut and layered too and it suited her. It might suit me at a pinch I thought, but I might keep the colour a little darker, go for a honey blonde. I mentioned this to Sid but he just mumbled. He's not one for fashion hints.

So what time is it now? My watch says

three-forty and at exactly three-thirty, Frank and Julie came out of their bungalow and into the garden. I slipped on my shoes, (can't be doing with slippers in the garden, after all I tell myself, their full name is 'carpet slippers' and you don't get that many carpets outside). So, I'd put on my shoes and raced round the side of the bungalow and into the back garden.

'Yoo-hoo, Julie, Frank.' (I said her name first so she didn't get the idea that I was too familiar with Frank.) They turned.

'I just wanted to ask you the name of your hairdre...' my voice came to an abrupt halt. I was face to face with Julie. Her blonde hair was lovely but it didn't really go with her five o'clock shadow. My eyes scanned down her body. She'd very muscley legs. Too muscley for the skirt she was wearing, it was too short. Her shoes were nice though, and I told her. They were ice blue, lattice leather design.

'Oh, Julie, I like those shoes, where did you get them from? I'd love a pair like that.'

When Julie answered her voice was deep. She'd fit easily into the bass section of a male voice choir, I thought. She kindly gave me the name of the shop but I don't think it was one that I would go to, people might get the wrong idea and it might upset Sid.

Frank smiled, 'She's lovely isn't she?'

I smiled back. I couldn't say yes and be totally convincing. I went back into the house. Sid was asleep, the paper creaking with every breath. I coughed. Sid didn't respond so I nudged him, then I whispered, 'you know when Frank said he was with the wrong woman in the bungalow in Wales? Well...'

I knew it wouldn't go any further, you see we don't gossip in the cul de sac.

2 THE CUL DE SAC AND MR CARVER

Beattie and I have been friends ever since me and Sid, moved into the cul de sac. She brought us a casserole, a 'welcome dish'. I learnt then what it was to live in the cul de sac. We all look out for each other. Beattie's still part of the 'welcoming group'. She's eighty now but once in a while her services are called for. Generally folk don't leave the cul de sac to make way for new arrivals, not under their own steam, anyway.

Beattie popped round to see me one morning recently. She was worried about one of our residents; Mr. Carver. He'd moved to the bungalow in 1978. His wife was alive then. Norma died two years ago and then Brian was on his own.

'He's looking frail,' Beattie said. I just 'Mmmed'. After all Brian's eighty-seven, so what can you expect?

'And,' she continued, 'he's not mowed his lawn for weeks. That front garden's a terrible state.

It'll let us down in the open gardens event next week. He'll have to get his act together.'

I can tell you, I was taken aback. You see as a rule, we help each other if we can. It's the way we are. And to think, we call Beattie, 'our welcoming queen'. Well, she doesn't get that name because she won't help people, it's exactly the opposite. She's turned helping people into an art form. I wondered if she was 'under the weather'.

'Would you like a coffee, Beattie?' I asked.

'Yes', she said, and then, 'You don't think I'm being too hard on him, do you, considering his age and all?'

' Beattie', I said, 'We've been friends for a long time and I know where I am with you. You speak your mind, but in this case I think we should be flexible. We don't want to upset anyone, not in the cul de sac. I remember when we first moved here, Beattie. You brought us that lovely casserole. Sid and I knew then that we'd made the right choice, but to be honest I'd never considered what could happen along the way, age and such, and Beattie, we're all heading in that direction.'

Beattie looked at me. I didn't know whether she was angry or not. She had very tiny eyes and wore very large glasses, (they covered most of her face) so you see how awkward it made things for me.

'I take it then that you think I am being harsh, but something has to be done' she said, We'll have to talk to Brian.'

She was right. Something would have to be done with Brian's garden before the 'open gardens' event.

'Let your Ray talk to Brian,' I suggested.
'Man to man, that's the best thing.'

'Ray doesn't want to do it. He suggested Sid.'

'That wouldn't be any good. Sid barely speaks to me.'

'What do we do then?'

'Couldn't your Ray just mow the lawn for Brian? That will give him the hint and then if he feels he needs more help he will let us know. We could prepare a rota in the meantime. I wouldn't mind helping and Sid can cut grass. He doesn't say much but he's a whizz with a lawnmower.'

Beattie's face lit up, and even through her glasses, I could see she was pleased. We spent the next ten minutes working on the rota and then after coffee we went door to door. We were pleased with the response. Julie and Frank (my neighbours) added their names to the list for mowing and weeding and then Julie said she, *'thought Brian had looked peaky the last time she had seen him,'* then added, ' I'm making a stew for dinner and I'll make sure there's enough over for Brian. You don't mind, do you Beattie?' Beattie said not. Julie smiled, 'I didn't want to step on your toes. Frank can take it round later. He can have a few minutes with him, just to make sure he's all right.'

Beattie and I looked at each other, 'meal rota' we said, and giving Julie our mumbled apologies, we went next door to my house and got out pen and paper again. I asked Beattie to stay for lunch but couldn't twist her arm. She said she'd pop back later for a cup of tea. It's like that in the cul de sac, we do things properly, 'morning coffee and afternoon tea'. Some traditions just aren't meant to be broken.

When Beattie returned it was nearly four o'clock. I said to her, 'I'd almost given up, thought you weren't coming.'

'Oh no, Rita. If that had been the case I'd have let you know. No, it's Ray. He's worried, about Brian.'

'But we've got that sorted, we've made rotas.'

'Yes, I know. But Ray's right. You see, we know his grass is long, but have we seen him? That's what Ray said, when did we last see him?'

'Well you've seen him Beattie. You told me so when you came round this morning.'

'I didn't.'

'You did. You said he looked frail.'

'Yes, but that didn't mean that I'd seen him recently.'

'When did you see him then?'

'Three weeks ago.'

'Did you speak to him?'

'Of course I did. I reminded him it was 'open gardens' coming up and he said he'd 'big plans'.'

'That doesn't sound like someone who wouldn't bother. What do you think has happened?'

'He could be dead,' she replied.

'We'll have to stop Julie taking the casserole. Drink your tea up and then we'll pop next door.'

Julie, as always, looked immaculate. Her clothes were very, very good. She liked a lot of

embroidery and was particularly fond of sequin
motifs. Her evening wear for the cul de sac New
Year Bash was breathtaking. She wore a long black
gown with a small fish tail at the back, all sequins
and diamante. It was low at the front but not too
low. It could easily have been worn by Dame
Shirley and not looked out of place. The 'Bash' was
the first 'big do' we'd organised but there'll be
more, there will. I said to Beattie at the time, 'It
seems as though these are going to be grand affairs,
no more sitting up with Jools Holland and a sweet
sherry.'

As we stepped into Julie's I said, 'It's Brian,
when did you last see him? Only we're wondering
if he's more than frail, more perhaps, not with us.'

'You think he might be dead?' Julie said.

We were still discussing the possibilities
when Frank said, 'I'll go round there now and
assess the situation, won't be long,' and with that he
was off.

He soon returned. 'What did you find?' Julie
asked.

'Nothing, can't see a thing. I went round the
back, the bed's made and not been slept in.'

'Did you check the hall, look through the
letterbox?' I asked.

'Yes. The only place I couldn't check was the
bathroom. The blind's down.'

''Phone the police,' Beattie said. 'They can
break in.'

Julie was on to the job in a tick. In some ways
she put me in mind of Katie Boyle, brusque and
efficient. I think it was the suit she was wearing. It

was very French and so chic.

The police were pretty quick and by five o'clock they were gaining access to Brian's bungalow. When they came outside they broke the good news to us, he wasn't there. The bungalow was empty. We were stunned. Where was Brian? And why didn't we know?

Anyway, as decided, the names on the rota cut his grass and weeded his borders. It wasn't just helping a neighbour, we also wanted to get things looking good for the 'open gardens' event, and that was now less than a week away.

Frank's garden was a picture, ours was passable. One or two of our plants had given up the ghost but Sid and I went along to the garden centre and bought some pots and summer bedding. When Sid had planted these up we grouped them in the 'failed spaces'. We always group pots. We find it looks so much better.

It was while we were grouping the pots in the front garden that I noticed a taxi pull up outside Brian's bungalow. I nudged Sid. He looked and said, 'That taxi, it's at Brian's.'

Sid and I watched. When Brian saw us he waved. We waved back, (we didn't want to stare, it reeks of impropriety) then carried on with the job in hand, the grouping of our pots. I did mention to Sid that I didn't think Brian looked frail or peaky to me. Sid didn't answer.

Later on I went round to Beattie's and asked her what we should do about the meal rota, she said,

'I think we should just leave it for now'.

So we did.

On the Friday before the 'open gardens' event, Bill, our cul de sac community leader, called round to see us. He wanted to check that we were all 'au fait' with everything and that we knew the drill, he said, 'and remember, check entry programmes. The programme has the *'cul de sac rose'* stamped on to signify payment. If it's not stamped, charge 'em two quid.'

Bill was ex-army and sometimes I think he got rather carried away with the idea of giving orders, but we wouldn't have done half the cul de sac events without his ideas. When he'd finished I asked, 'Is Brian's garden opening? Only he told Beattie he'd 'big plans.'

'Doubtful, but I think we'll see him later.'

I was disappointed Bill hadn't said more.

At the end of the 'open gardens' day we always gather at Bill's for a take away meal and Buck's Fizz. It's Bill's way of saying 'thank you'. Bill's bungalow has a conservatory, so it makes good sense to go there.

While chatting I was glancing round. There was no sign of Brian. I mentioned it to Bill, but he just said, 'he'll be along later.'

When Brian arrived, and made his way into the conservatory I could see he had a woman with him. And as he began to speak, the woman looked at him and smiled. She was younger than most everyone in the conservatory, only mid sixties, tops.

'Hello', Brian began, 'I wasn't looking forward to mowing the lawns when I got back, but everything's been done for me, thank you.'

Brian looked at the woman by his side and smiled. She smiled back. Brian carried on, 'I must introduce the lady who made me leave my gardening to you for a week or two, please, meet Primrose.'

She seemed pleasant and Brian looked remarkably dapper. Beattie looked across and said,

'Brian, you told me you'd 'big plans', and as far as I can see nothing in your garden's changed.'

'Quite right. The only big plan I had was marrying Primrose. I couldn't say anything in case I was refused at the last hurdle, but as you can see, I wasn't.'

Brian took Primrose's hand and squeezed it affectionately.

At this point Bill stepped forward.

'I think we should congratulate the happy couple in the traditional way. I'll go and get some champagne.'

As I've said, Primrose does seem pleasant and I think she will take to cul de sac life quite well, and during the little celebration at Bill's, we found out that she plays Mah Jong. Well, you won't be surprised when I tell you that there happens to be a Mah Jong league in the cul de sac. We play on a Monday afternoon. The winner has the 'Magic Pagoda', for a week. It's a pale-blue colour, and quite heavy for its size.

No one really knows where it came from. There was a suspicion that Edna and Harold had something to do with it, but no one's really sure, and Edna and Harold have never said anything in the affirmative, so we just don't know. What I can say, is that it has just become another of our cul de sac traditions. It's something we can all aspire to. And if you don't win, there are always the fortune cookies that Bill brings along every Monday.

Now where does he get them from? That's another thing we don't know.

3 JOAN, THICK SANDWICHES AND SUN-SEEKERS

Joan (famous for her sandwiches for cul de sac events) worked in the local charity shop on a Tuesday, the same day as me. We always had a good chat and a catch up. Even though we both lived in the cul de sac it was the only time we knew that our paths would definitely cross. Well, you can't gossip at Mah Jong.

On this particular Tuesday Joan had opened up the shop at 10 am, I didn't arrive until eleven. Anyway, as soon as I put my feet through the shop door I could see something was amiss.

'Joan', I said, 'Whatever's the matter? You look as though you've got the weight of the world on your shoulders.'

'Rita, I think you've hit the nail on the head. I don't know what to do or who to turn to.'

'Let me take my coat off,' I said, 'And you can tell me.'

I was glad Joan wanted to have a chat. There was something I had to talk to her about, and this would give me an opportunity to broach the subject.

It had been noted that the last time Joan had made sandwiches for a cul de sac event, the bread was cut in rather thick slices. Usually Joan's sandwiches are perfect, neat little triangles, crusts removed of course. This last lot were so thick, I was just glad I had my own teeth.

When I came back on the shop floor Joan smiled but I could see from her demeanour that she had a real problem and it was obviously bothering her.

'Has it been a busy morning?' I asked.

'So-so', she answered.

'Shall I make us some coffee?' I offered, thinking to myself, *'a drink's usually the best aid to sorting out problems'*.

'That would be nice,' Joan replied.

When I brought the tray out of the staff room it did look pretty. I used our best China cups. I know they were tea cups but I didn't think it would be too much of a problem. They had been left over from a set. The design was called 'Braganza' and it was a pretty little floral design of blue and grey. I liked it anyway.

Joan was quiet at first. I had to prompt her to set her going.

'Well?' I said. Then she opened up.

'I don't really know where to start. Do you remember Gladys and Ernie moving in next door to us when Ralph died?'

'Yes.'

'They seemed a lovely couple don't you think?'

'Yes. Beattie said they were really appreciative when she called round with the 'welcome casserole'.

'Oh yes, she told me that. Said that Fred and me would get on with them like a house on fire. And we did.' Joan looked dejected at this point.

'So what's happened? It can't be the garden. They keep it very well. Are they loud? Because if they are, Bill should be told. He would go round and have a word with them.'

'No, it's nothing like that.'

Joan looked worried, and now we'd customers in the shop. I moved the tray out of sight.

Freda and Jessie had come in. We knew their names even though they didn't live in the cul de sac. They were part of a band of regulars who came into the shop week after week. They were usually miserable. Nothing was ever right. On occasion they had been known to return goods. I ask you? Return goods to a charity shop? We were always wary when we saw them come in but when you go face to face with Joe Public you soon realise that it takes all sorts.

When they'd gone, I looked at Joan,

'Coffee'll be cold now, shall I make a fresh one or do you just want to carry on?'

Joan looked at her watch. It was a quarter to one.

'I finish at half past today. Sylvia will be here soon. Muriel wants me to show her the ropes, as she'll be covering for me when I have the physio treatments for my foot over the next few weeks.'

'Well, there's not that much that Sylvia doesn't know anyway. She's been working with us quite closely these last few weeks,' I said.

'Yes, but if my foot doesn't respond to treatment, the physio says I may have to give up the shop work. He says that the standing isn't doing me any good. Sylvia could become a permanent fixture.'

That last remark didn't bear thinking about. Sylvia was a lot younger than the rest of the volunteers. I was hoping that Betty and Beattie might be given more hours. Anyway, we'd just have to wait and see. For the moment I needed to help a friend through a problem.

Joan continued, 'I suppose I should just carry on and then you can advise me.'

There was a slight pause, I think Joan was searching for the right words. I tried to prompt her.

'Joan?'

She carried on. 'As I said, it was great when they first moved in, but it was winter and very cold.'

I agreed. The winter had been very long and very cold.

She carried on again, 'But then came the spring and it was quite warm. I'd see Gladys and we'd pass the time of day, she works you know, at the vet's in town. She's on reception.'

'Likes animals then, that's always a good

sign.'

'Yes, I suppose,' Joan replied. 'Anyway now the summer's with us and things have changed, but not for the better. I feel as though my world has been turned upside down, everything's on its head. It's Ernie, he's the problem. He's not behaving like a cul de sac er. He's making things very difficult.'

I knew it was serious. It was twelve fifty-five pm. We'd have to get to the bottom of things before one fifteen. Sylvia was always prompt, if not early. I looked at Joan. 'Can Gladys shed any light on the problem?'

'I hope not,' she said and laughed. 'What he does happens in the back garden. You know our hedge is only three foot high, and Fred is very particular about keeping it clipped. I was in the kitchen when I first noticed it. It was as soon as the good weather started. Ernie would...' Joan paused, 'Ernie would reveal himself.'

'On the cul de sac?' I asked.

'In his garden,' Joan replied. 'He would walk down the drive with only a towel to... to hide his mystery.'

I must admit I was teetering on the edge. The edge that was the barrier between stunned and shocked. Joan looked at me, 'Well Rita, what do you think?'

I coughed. And then Sylvia appeared. It was twenty past one.

'All right ladies, you can go when you like, I'm here.'

'I'm here until two-fifteen, Joan's on until half past one, and she's got to make sure you know the ropes,' I said.

Sylvia smiled. She's rather brash if the truth be told but then we don't know where she's from. Muriel our manageress, is the only one who knows and she's not telling. Anyway, as you could imagine Joan was still in a state. As she prepared to leave she looked me in the eye. 'Any thoughts Rita?'

'Yes, come over to me at three o'clock. We'll give it some more thought then.'

I could see that this pleased Joan and even though we don't gossip in the cul de sac, there's no harm in a chat to help a friend.

When Joan arrived we went straight into the lounge. I'd dispatched Sid to the library. He wasn't much of a reader but I'd asked him to collect a book for me. I hadn't actually reserved a book but well, I was thinking on my feet. Joan sat down and I made a pot of Earl Grey. Then I began, 'Did you speak to Ernie at all when you saw him?'

'No,' Joan said and flushed pink. 'But there's more. I've noticed that when he gets in the back garden,' at this point Joan took a large drink of tea.

'Yes?' I said, 'What does he do in the garden?'

'Rita', she said, 'He removes his towel.'

'Does he do it often?' I asked.

'I've seen him on a few occasions.'

'Mmm' I said. I could see this needed to be given some more thought. We'd have to pacify both parties; Joan whose sensitivities were being upset and Ernie who obviously needed to be taken aside and talked too, somehow.

When Joan had left, I was the one in a tizz. Sid came back from the library, 'They didn't know you'd ordered a book,' he said.

I smiled and said, 'Thanks Sid. I'll sort it out next time I'm in town.'

I prepared our evening meal in silence. Every part of Joan's story playing over in my head. We'd not had anything like this in the cul de sac before.

Over dinner Sid asked me why I was so quiet. I told him I was thinking. By the time the meal was over I knew what I must do. I would go and see Bill. He was, after all ex-army. He would know what to do and he'd be able to speak to Ernie. Yes, that was the solution.

Bill kept Ernie under surveillance for a few weeks that summer. He 'holed' himself up at Joan and Fred's. And as it turned out he didn't need to speak to Ernie. It was all quite innocent really, as you'd expect in the cul de sac. Ernie was nothing more than a sun worshipper. Under that towel he wore to spare Joan's blushes as he walked down the drive, he wore a pair of teeny, tiny speedos. Joan hadn't noticed these and had Ernie down as a naturist.

So, it's all sorted out now. Fred's letting the hedge grow another couple of feet. It won't block anyone's light and everyone will be happy.

Meanwhile, Joan is sporting a very fashionable pair of designer specs and her sand-wiches are back on track.

4 THE CUL DE SACERS GO SWIMMING

Joan was fully recovered from the 'naturist' disaster. Once she'd been to the opticians she was a new woman. Well, it was a relief to everyone in the cul de sac, and after the surprise wedding, things were settling down nicely.

Brian's wife, Primrose, was continuing to do well in the Mah Jong group and was a very good player, (as I expected) and continued to win the 'Magic Pagoda' regularly.

It was Primrose who was the driving force behind the 'morning coffee club'.

Our week was very full with activities but Primrose thought it would be a good opportunity for us, (the ladies of the cul de sac), to get together and bond. 'Bond', was one of Primrose's words, she said that they did it a lot in her office, had bonding sessions, and Gladys said she did a lot of it at Mr McGluskey's. He was the local vet. She said that now she was at Mr McGluskey's, and particularly now she was on reception for a few hours a week, that they often had weekly bonding meetings. They would, she said, stay in the evening, when surgery had finished and have fish and chips. I said that I didn't think that sounded very hygienic, but Gladys said I was missing the point.

Anyway, to get back to the Monday coffee mornings, they were a great success; and we moved round the bungalows, to make it fair.

It was when Julie was hosting the coffee morning that a new suggestion was made. Primrose had started 'Swim-aerobics', she said, at the local pool, and she was really pushing it to us as a good form of exercise.

'It's very gentle,' she said. 'Nothing too strenuous.'

'What do you mean exactly by, *very gentle*?' Julie asked.

I was surprised by Julie's question. She was the last person I thought would be bothered by the thought of any kind of exercise. She was so sturdy and well built. I said as much to her.

'Oh, I'm a martyr to a catalogue of aches and pains,' she said.

'It's never obvious', I said.

'I don't like people to know. I'd much rather keep it to myself.'

'You do very well,' I replied. 'and you're such a vital part of cul de sac activities.' Julie just smiled.

Primrose continued, 'You've nothing to worry about, Julie. The teacher caters for everyone and if you find one thing too difficult or if it's in any way too much for you, you just sit that exercise out.

Nobody at all is under any pressure. And they're a great group. In the changing rooms afterwards, we have a laugh and a joke discussing the highs and the lows of the session, and then we all go for a coffee in the leisure centre cafe before we leave.'

'So the changing rooms are communal, then?' I asked.

'Yes,' Primrose replied, 'but don't let that worry you, just bring a beach towel if you're nervous. It's great fun, honest.'

I must admit to having reservations, but everyone else seemed very keen.

The next Wednesday at 11.15am, Primrose, Julie, Beattie, Joan, Gladys and myself, turned up at the Leisure Centre for 'Swim-aerobics'.

It started out very well, once we were all in the pool. The first hurdle was to get Joan in some water.

Without her glasses on her vision was limited and she struggled to put her naked foot on the pool-side step; and that was with her being ably assisted by Gladys and myself.

Elaine Grainger who ran the class, was as Primrose said, very nice. She also reminded me of Jackie Wilson, the school hockey captain, way back when I was in my third year at senior school. Yes, Elaine and Jackie Wilson could have been sisters. In fact, they were so much alike that I began to find it difficult to separate the two in my head. Anyway, given Joan's predicament, Elaine suggested we make use of the pool-side hoist. Joan wasn't too keen at first but she eventually saw that it was the only way she would get into the pool, and then of course, Elaine pointed out that most of the class had been waiting in the pool for ten minutes, and, she emphasised, 'the session is one hour, no more, no less.'

Gladys and myself helped to get Joan secure, and then with the help of a very nice young man from Leisure and Recreation, Joan was in, and once unleashed and in full possession of her sea legs, we could all begin.

Primrose had said it was gentle, and it was. Elaine stood to the shallow end of the pool. We girls, (I use this term loosely as the youngest in the group was Primrose), formed a circle, an arm's length gap left between you and your partners, so as to avoid 'bumping'.

Elaine showed us the first exercise with a brisk demonstration. Marching on the spot, knees brought up as high as you can, for three minutes. I marched as though I'd been born to it, we all did. I don't think any of us had lifted our knees so high in a long time. We stopped when Elaine gave the signal, a raised arm and one long blow on the whistle that hung on a lanyard around her neck.

Next exercise, propellers with the arms; first one arm then the other, and then both together; the direction was indicated by Elaine. I felt I was born again. It was just as Primrose had said, and we were all enjoying it. Elaine even commented on how much her new set of 'water babies' were adding to the group. The Head of Leisure would be pleased she said, 'as all services were under threat'. It was a situation we in the cul de sac were all too aware of, and Julie had for some time now been volunteering at the local library one evening a week. Her volunteering coincided with Frank's darts night at the Black Dog; it was lucky that the late night at the library and darts night were on a Thursday, but Julie had one mantra that she adhered to, and that was, 'failing to plan is planning to fail'. *What else could you expect from a cul de sac lady?* I thought, and that's what Julie was, through and through.

It was during the next exercise that I realised I wasn't feeling quite myself. We had all started to march from the shallow end of the pool to the deep end of the pool, (as if treading water), with floats supporting us. These floats were like huge brightly coloured worms that went across our chests and under our arms. I started off fine, I was keeping up with the crowd. I glanced across at Primrose, she smiled at me and mouthed, 'ok?' I nodded in the affirmative. I was lying. Primrose passed me, Gladys and Julie passed me, even Joan who couldn't see a hand in front of her passed me. I looked for Beattie. She was heading for the shallow end of the pool. I turned and started to take her course.

'Wait for me, Beattie,' I called. Elaine looked at us.

'Ladies, ladies, whatever's the matter?'

'I'm sorry Elaine, this bit's beyond me. I'll sit it out if you don't mind.'

'All right you two, we'll be back down in a minute or two and then you can carry on. We'll do some warming down exercises.'

I smiled. There and then I decided this would

be my first and last visit to Swim-aerobics, I would have to find some other way to bond.

'What do you reckon Beattie, is it your cup of tea?'

'It could be. I like the water, but perhaps not for an hour.'

'I think I agree with you. I shall have to let Primrose know of course, but I don't think I'm cut out for this.'

The rest of the group were returning to the shallow end.

'Ladies, just take a minute or two to get your breath back.' Elaine looked around the group. 'Well ladies, I must say I'm extremely pleased with our new recruits. I think for first timers you've all done well to keep up with the rest of the group.'

The stalwarts of the group looked across and applauded us. I think it was more to gee us on than from any thoughts they might be fostering as to how good we were.

'Right ladies, some gentle warming down movements now, to the side of the pool please and hold the bar.'

Elaine looked at us, 'Now all ready, hold on and bend those knees, soles of your feet to the wall of the pool, now hold it, now lean back, gently, but as far as you can. That's it, hold it for, two, three, four, five, now slowly stand up. Don't you feel lovely and relaxed?'

'No,' I said.

'Whatever do you mean?' Elaine questioned.

'My legs feel like jelly. I don't think I'll ever be able to walk un-aided again.'

'Of course you will. You've just used muscles that you didn't know you had, and now they're letting you know. You'll be fine after a warm shower.'

'I don't think I'll be able to get out of the pool, my legs are wobbly, really wobbly.'

'Don't worry, we'll use the hoist, we'll have to use it for Joan, anyway,' Elaine said.

'And me,' said Beattie, 'I'll need the hoist.'

'And I think it would be safer for me,' said Gladys.

'I'll try the steps,' Julie said, but I could see by her gait that it wouldn't be any use.

The session had gone on for well over the hour by the time we had all got out. There wasn't time to have a laugh and a joke in the changing room. There wasn't time for a coffee in the cafe afterwards.

Primrose 'phoned for a taxi. She didn't mention Swim-aerobics again, but we all know she still goes. It's like that when you live in a cul de sac.

5 BILL'S CLIFFHANGER AND OTHER MEETINGS

As far as I know, our cul de sac co-ordinator and all round good guy, ex-army man Bill, has never been married. I'd never asked him of course, that would border on impropriety and in the cul de sac we try to steer away from that sort of thing. Anyway, impropriety out of the way, I'd never noticed any sign of a female presence in his bungalow; not in the decor nor in any items left around the rooms. And one thing there was a certain lack of was photographs. In Bill's bungalow there were no family photographs. Sid told me it was none of my business what people had in their homes, it was entirely up to them. That, I thought, was surprising coming from Sid, as he doesn't say much at all and for him to venture an opinion, I thought, was quite remarkable.

'He can keep what he likes in his house,' I said. 'What I'm remarking on is that there's no evidence of a female in his past.'

'Perhaps he hadn't got the time, he'd be away a lot in the army.'

'Yes, you could have a point there.'

We were getting ready to go round to Bill's for the quarterly meeting of the cul de sac group. Bill organised these meetings with military precision and he steered the agenda through without ever veering from the points listed. No one was allowed to deviate. He was a dedicated chairman of our group and we all thought there would never be another Bill. The saying, 'when they made him they threw away the mould,' was often heard when people spoke of our chairman.

When we arrived at Bill's bungalow for 20.00 hours, he already had the light on in his conservatory, (that was where the meetings were often held). We all went through and sat down, agendas were placed on all the seats. I had a quick glance down the list. I noticed one of the headings, 6.ii 'Criminal activity'.

I nudged Sid, 'Look at this, on the agenda, criminal activity. I wonder what's...'

I was stopped in my tracks, Bill spoke, 'You know we don't discuss items before the meeting Rita. There has to be a good degree of protocol or the whole group could fall apart, end up in tatters, now, places please.'

Sufficiently chided, I placed the agenda on my knee and got a pen from my bag. Bill began, 'It's just leaving five past the hour, so I will declare the meeting open, are there any apologies for absence?'

There were none. The meeting continued.

The first items on the agenda were the usual run of the mill type things that tend to get discussed at every meeting, for example, how much the last fund raising event had made, the state of the gardens, was everyone keeping on top of the outside maintenance of their properties, general items that were of no interest to anyone outside of our cul de sac.

Item 6.ii, would probably be of no interest to anyone outside of our cul de sac either, but I couldn't wait to get there.

Item 6.i was cleared away in a flash. It was thought that local hooligans (not that we have many anywhere near the cul de sac) were throwing litter from waste bins and that the papers and food trays were finding their way into the gardens. At the last meeting it was decided that Bill would 'stake out' the offending litter bins, to catch whoever was responsible red-handed. Bill was pleased to report back that we hadn't had an influx of undesirables to the cul de sac, but that we had over-zealous squirrels. In the light of that it was decided that Sid and Frank would empty the bins a minimum of twice a week and see if the problem could be alleviated.

'Now', Bill said, 'On to a more serious matter. I have to bring it to everyone's attention that there has been a spate of burglaries in the adjoining streets to our cul de sac. Our local police officer, Ged Thwaite has asked me to spread the word. He says that forewarned is forearmed and that all of us need to be extra diligent; don't just nip out and leave windows open, even the tiniest window can make way for a thief. Take care if you leave your cars on the drive over night, make sure they're locked and that you know where the keys are. Keep an eye out for one another. We don't want this criminal activity to spread to our cul de sac.'

'Do we know who's been burgled or what's been taken?' I asked.

'I don't think it would have been right for Ged to give any details such as those. He just wanted to let us know what's happening under our very noses.'

'Thanks for that Bill,' I said. 'It makes you wonder though, I must say.'

Bill moved swiftly on, 'Right, item 7, any other business?'

There wasn't. That only left the time and date of the next meeting, well it was always at Bill's and it would be three months on.

I went with Beattie to the kitchen and we brewed up. We always finished the meetings with a cup of tea and a 'Thin Arrowroot'. They were Bill's favourite biscuit.

'What do you think about that, then?' I asked Sid when we arrived back home.

'What do you mean?' he asked.

I might have mentioned before that Sid's a man of few words but I thought his remark, even for him, a little simplistic.

'We've just been to our cul de sac meeting and

discovered there's a crime wave happening on the through roads. I'd have thought you'd have had an opinion about it. We don't want to be burgled do we?'

'Look, it's late love. We've talked enough about everything tonight at Bill's. Let's just sleep on it. All we can do is as Bill's advised us all, we have to be extra vigilant.'

'And that's it, is it?' I asked. 'We could all be murdered in our beds.'

'Rita, that's taking things a little too far. Try and keep things in perspective. Anyway, as I've said, I'm off to bed, good night love.'

And that was it. That was all I could get from Sid. If he didn't want to talk no amount of cajoling was going to make him spout forth. I knew this from experience, but it had never made things any easier for me. I was a talkative person, I liked my questions answered. I wanted all the i's dotted and all the t's crossed.

I made myself a cup of tea and sat in the kitchen, thinking things over. When I went to bed Sid was already asleep. I couldn't settle. I sat for a moment looking out of the bedroom window, as discreetly as I could of course. I didn't want to draw attention to myself, or my bungalow for that matter. I didn't want any undesirables catching sight of me and perhaps taking action because they assumed I was on to them. Life in a cul de sac bungalow had just become difficult. I felt sick. Those were words that I never thought I'd hear myself think. It didn't stop there. *If we had stayed on two floors*, I thought to myself, *then, we would have had the ground floor and a flight of stairs between us and the ones we wanted to avoid.* That alone would have given me the feeling of safety that I didn't have now. I sat in the old Lloyd Loom and covered myself with a rug. I didn't feel safe at all after tonight's meeting, I decided that I would spend the night here, nodding whenever my eyelids forced me; and see if I could report anything to Bill in the morning.

I was up with the larks, well, probably a little while before the larks or any other type of day-light bird and I had had my breakfast and several cups of tea before Sid emerged.

'You're up early love', he said, 'But from the look of you, you don't look like you've slept at all.'

'I haven't, not really. I kept watch from our bedroom window. I wondered whether I'd see anything that might be of interest to Bill. This whole crimewave thing has really got to me.'

'We haven't got a crimewave. Bill said that it's on the through roads. I don't really think we've anything to worry about. Bill was just letting us know, that's all.'

'He might have been *'letting us know,'* as you say, but it's worried me.'

'You shouldn't be losing sleep over it, though. It's not worth it. You'll make yourself ill.'

'Maybe, but I can't help it, Sid. I'm going over when the time's reasonable and I'll have a word with Bill, see if he knows anything more.'

'Rita, I really think you're over-reacting.

How can he possibly know anymore yet? It's only hours since we were at his house at the meeting and he told us what was going on.'

'I know. But I'm going round anyway.'

'I thought you would.'

'Rita, come in. Is everything all-right?'

'Yes, thanks; well maybe not everything.'

'Cup of coffee?'

'No thanks Bill. I've only popped round to see if you've had any news about the crimewave?'

'Hardly. The meeting only finished twelve hours ago. And as I mentioned the break-ins have been on the through roads. I don't think it will really affect us. You're always safer in a cul de sac, that's the thinking, anyway.'

'I was beginning to wish I still had a flight of stairs between me and the bad guys. Sid said I was taking things to heart too much, but I just wanted to pop round. I've been up most of the night 'on watch' as it were. I didn't notice anything apart from a few cats and a fox making its way home.'

'It's very laudable Rita, but there's no need to lose sleep over it, I can assure you of that. You've really nothing to worry about, believe me.'

'Ok. But if you do hear of anything, you will let us know, won't you? It'll make me feel much safer. It'll give me peace of mind if I'm kept up to speed.'

'I'll let you know if there's anything to report; in the meantime as they say on Crimewatch, *'don't have nightmares.'*

Sid was reading the paper when I arrived back home. He looked up as I walked into the lounge.

'What did Bill say, did he know anything?'

'He said what you'd said he would.'

Sid smiled and carried on reading the paper. That was the end of our conversation for the time being. I decided to 'phone Beattie.

'No Beattie, couldn't get anything new from him. But I can tell you it's got me worried.'

'I'm not worried as such, but I've decided to do what Bill says and be more vigilant and make sure I do the sensible thing and not nip out and leave windows and doors open.'

'Yes, that does seem the thing to do.'

'Something has happened today though, that I haven't seen in a while. We've had a police presence on the cul de sac.'

'We have?'

'Yes.'

'When was that?'

'About ten o'clock.'

'Really? That was when I was in Bill's. I'm beginning to wish I hadn't gone round now.'

'They were only walking round the cul de sac. They didn't call anywhere.'

'They? There was more than one of them, then?'

'Yes, but only just. There were two of them. Only looked like young girls. But I guess that's what that saying means.'

'What's that?'

'Oh you must know it Rita, the one that says, *you know you're getting older when the police officers start looking young.'*

'Oh that. Yes, I'd forgotten; but I suppose that was from the days when the police were all men. You've just said yourself that they only looked like young girls. I don't know which is worse, getting older or having to resort to girls to sort out the crimewave. I will keep an eye out again tonight, perhaps not all night but at least it'll make me feel safer.'

'I think you're taking it far too seriously, it's not a crimewave, it's just one or two break-ins, and they haven't happened on the cul de sac. Cul de sac's, so the statistics show are the safest form of road to live on. It's all in the government figures.'

'And we believe everything we're told, do we?'

'Maybe not all the time, but in this case, and on the cul de sac, I think you shouldn't take it all to heart, that's all I'm saying.'

My chat to Beattie hadn't helped ease the issue. I couldn't think straight so I decided to walk into the town. Sid had some roses that he'd said needed attention so I thought it was a good idea to get out of the way in any case. Sid didn't mind help in the garden, but what he did mind was when I tried to advise him on rose care. The decision was made. I reminded Sid about security as I left. He didn't answer.

When I arrived back home I felt much

better; being in town amongst the hustle and bustle had helped me get things into perspective, which was more or less what Sid, Bill and Beattie had advised. And on the plus side, I'd splashed out and bought a new jacket from 'Misty Blue', one of the most up-market shops on the high street. I'd enjoyed coffee and chat with the great and the good in the newest branch of 'Bean There'. I was glad I'd made the time for it.

A quick glance at the roses and I could see Sid had been making headway. The rose bed in the front garden was immaculate. One thing I didn't like the look of as I walked up the drive however, was the fact that he'd left all his gardening tools on full view and he was nowhere in sight. I could feel what I supposed to be my blood pressure, start to rise. I went through the back door, which was unlocked and saw that Sid was on the 'phone. That explained a few things then, he must have rushed in to answer the 'phone, not had time to move any of his things. I nodded to him and then put my shopping in the kitchen and went out and brought in his gardening tools. I put them on newspaper by the back door. I heard the 'phone click as he replaced the receiver. 'I'll put the kettle on, 'I said. 'I expect you're ready for a drink.'

'I don't think we'll have time. That was Bill on the 'phone; he wants as many of us as can get round, to go over to his house ASAP. I'll just go and get changed out of these gardening clothes.'

'Did he give any explanation?'

'He said there's been a development in the rash of break-ins and that we ought to know about it.'

As we filed into Bill's conservatory I could see that we were nearly all present. We all knew that Primrose and Brian were going away for a few days so their absence was no surprise. When we were all seated, Bill said, 'I'm sorry to have to get you all here at short notice but I thought you'd all like to know that there's been a development. I've had my car taken off the drive in broad daylight.'

I looked at Sid. 'But you were out doing the rose bed, didn't you see anything?'

'I had to go inside, I wasn't there all the time.'

'I suppose then, that gives us some idea of a time when the theft took place, at least.'

'Good thinking, Rita,' Bill said.

'Did they take anything else? I know having your car taken is enough, but did they cause any damage to anything or take anything from the garden shed?'

'No, it was just the car. And, and... the funny thing is they didn't take everything that was in the car.'

'Whatever do you mean?' I said.

'They removed my Cliff Richard cds and placed them neatly on the porch step. There were six of them. Anyway, that doesn't matter, but what a strange thing to do. I mentioned it to the police constable who called round, but he didn't think it was relevant.'

'Do they think it's connected to the break-ins on the through roads?' Beattie asked.

'No, they don't seem to think there's any connection.'

Julie looked up, 'It seems an odd thing to do. Have you annoyed any local youth lately? You know they can get a bit cheeky and to me it seems more like a prank than anything else. Had you left the keys inside it then?'

'You sound very much like the young policeman who came round to take the details. Yes, I had inadvertently left the keys in the car. A momentary lapse of concentration.'

'And have you annoyed any young folk recently?'

'Julie, I'm ex-army. I probably annoy people on most days of my life.'

There was a knock at the door, Bill went to answer it.

'It's odd isn't it, leaving his cds on the porch step,' I said.

'That's why I think it's kids.' Julie said. 'Bill's a lovely man, but I bet some young people find him heavy going. He could've upset someone and not even realised that he's done it. I bet a pound to a penny that his car turns up in an hour or two. Some young lad will have done it for devilment.'

Bill returned. 'Well, good news. That was a PCSO, or for the uninitiated, a Police Community Support Officer. They've found my car. It was left with the keys in at the back of Blair's dry cleaners. When Jack Blair came back to his shop this afternoon he couldn't get in his parking space. No one in any of the shops had parked their car at the back and hey presto! It turns out to be mine. So, thank you all for coming round at such short notice but I think the panic's over and I'm off to collect my car. But all of you; please do watch out and be vigilant, it isn't over yet, this isn't the bigger picture that we're looking at, this is just the snap-shot. Now, I must ask you all to leave quite briskly as PCSO Sophie is going to escort me down to the station.'

'I must say Bill seems very cheerful all of a sudden, for someone who's just gone through the trauma of having their car stolen and their Cliff cds left neatly on the porch step.'

Sid didn't answer me, well not directly at any rate, he just said that he'd better get changed and go and finish in the garden.

Things in the cul de sac settled down and there was little or no talk of a crimewave and break-ins. I was beginning to feel a little more calm again with one level living and had stopped the night time vigils. A few weeks further down the line and we were reliably informed by the local paper that, *'the crime wave that has caused distress in the local community is now at its end. Two men, aged nineteen and twenty-nine, are in police custody and have admitted to twelve counts of theft.'*

'That's a huge relief, isn't it.' I said to Sid, when we were having our morning coffee, 'They've caught the ones responsible for the break-ins.'

'I always knew they would. I told you, you

were worrying too much.'

'I should've listened, it would have saved me all those sleepless nights. Still, all's well that ends well.'

The next meeting of the cul de sac group at Bill's was as per usual. By that I mean that nothing out of the ordinary had happened in the cul de sac. The crimewave had been and gone. The only thing that was any different was that the young PCSO Sophie was there. She was going to give us all a pep talk on crime prevention.

'What's happened to Ged Thwaite, then?' I asked. 'He usually attends the meetings for us when there's a security issue to be talked about.'

'He's moving on to pastures new,' Bill said. 'But we're not to feel alarmed; we have the lovely Sophie here who'll tell us all we want to know. She's our new point of contact.'

'But she's not a real policewoman. Aren't we having a real police presence on our streets anymore?'

'That's just what I was wondering,' Julie said, 'But I didn't like to mention it.'

Sophie stood up. 'I'm as official as any other officer in the police force. I can do all the things that regular officers do, and you get two and half of me, you only had one Ged Thwaite.'

'So it's to do with cut backs, isn't it? We haven't the funding for a permanent police presence. It's the big society - we're all in it together, isn't it?' I said.

'If you want to put it like that, it is,' Sophie

replied, 'but I will do whatever it takes and whatever's in my powers to safeguard the community. I am reliable. And I have extra man power, as I said, you get two and a half with me. By that I mean myself and Rob Andrews full time and our newest recruit Zena Holmes will be joining our happy band when she's finished training, but she'll only be on call fourteen hours a week.'

'I can vouch for everything that Sophie's said. I've met both Rob and Zena and I think we're jolly lucky to have them,' Bill said. He turned and looked at Sophie, 'After all, this is the officer who helped me retrieve my stolen car.'

'Yes, I suppose so,' I said.

I noticed Sophie as she turned and smiled at Bill. I didn't say anything but I thought, *this is Brian and Primrose all over again.*

I noticed Sophie on the cul de sac quite a few times over the coming weeks. She was keeping to her word at any rate, I thought, and making her PCSO presence felt. And in a funny way it did give you a feeling of security seeing her there on the street and knowing that if you wanted her she was only a 'phone call away.

Rob Andrews was a nice young man as well. He was friendly and didn't mind spending a minute or two talking to you when he met you on the street, and something that Beattie and I rather liked, he'd started popping into the charity shop on a Tuesday morning when we were in volunteering and would have a cup of coffee with us. It added a new dimension to our lives. The only one we hadn't met was Zena, but that would only be a matter of time.

The next cul de sac meeting at Bill's was scheduled and we all knew that it would be a lengthy meeting. The autumn meeting was always a long one as we discussed our next events and this usually involved the New Year's Eve get together and the planning for the carol singing. The carol singing wasn't confined to the cul de sac of course, it was us cul de sacers who went elsewhere to sing and raise money for a local charity. The popular choice of venue was the shopping arcade in town. The precinct management were usually quite amenable and as there was a lot of *'footfall'*, as Bill called it, we managed to raise quite substantial amounts, and as it was a Christmas event, we all enjoyed taking part. When the meeting was finally over, Beattie and I went into the kitchen to make the drinks. I could see Beattie was itching to tell me something.

'Rita, I don't know how I've managed to keep quiet, have you noticed anything?'

'Like what?'

'Bill and Sophie, they're very pally. I've seen her with Bill in town. It's terrible, he's so much older than she is, in fact, he's...'

'Ladies, put another cup and saucer out if you wouldn't mind, we've got an extra one for tea, Sophie's joining us.'

'Right Bill.' I said.

Bill went back into the conservatory.

'See what I mean, ' Beattie said, 'and he's blatant with it, having her back here for tea, and us all being here as well.'

'Well it is his house, I suppose he can invite whoever he likes.'

'I thought he was so proper as well, him being ex-army, and all.'

'I know what you mean, but it really has nothing to do with us, let's just let sleeping dogs lie and make the tea.'

I put an extra cup and saucer out and Beattie poured the tea while I got out the *Thin Arrowroot* biscuits. I'd no sooner completed the task than Bill appeared again, 'Better make it two extra cups, Rob's turned up now,' and he laughed quietly and left us again.

'This is getting to be a joke,' Beattie said. 'The burglars can all get on with it now, everyone from the local police is in Bill's conservatory.'

When Beattie and I got back into the conservatory everyone was in party mood. We wondered what we'd missed. I put the tray down on the low table and Beattie handed the biscuits round. I sat down next to Sid, he smiled at me. 'Just wait 'til you hear,' he said.

Bill stood up. 'Listen everyone, Rita and Beattie have missed out by being so good as to brew up for us all, but I can't let an occasion like this go by without an announcement of some sort, and an obligatory glass of champagne, which as you good people know, I always have on ice, but first the announcement that Rita and Beattie missed; our young friends Sophie and Rob have just announced their engagement. Yes, they're going to be married and they wanted us to be the first to know. Frank, you come with me and help me un-cork the champagne, Sid, you know where the glasses are.'

And that was how the meeting ended, on a particularly happy note, I thought.

When I spoke to Beattie the next day, she was a little put out because she'd seen more in the friendship of Sophie and Bill than there was to see. But as I'd said at the time, *he can invite whoever he likes to his home;* but I didn't mention that I'd thought of Brian and Primrose when I'd first seen them together; that would have been tittle-tattle, and we don't do that, not in the cul de sac.

6 GET AHEAD, GET A HAT

The walking group wasn't exactly a cul de sac affair but we *cul de sacers* provided most of the members, so in a way we felt like part owners, truth be told. The group got together on the first and third Sunday of the month to do a pre-planned walk. We met outside the Cherry Cup Cake cafe on the high street at 12.30 pm, and headed off from there. All the walks were fairly local and on the shortish side, (two hours max). This left us plenty of time to get a drink before the cafe closed at four o'clock. And, another consideration of course, was church, an afternoon meeting allowed those of us of faith, to attend church in the morning and still be out in time for the walk. Those of no faith had a lie in. It was a win, win situation.

Of course, the faith thing wasn't uppermost in our minds', as Bill was heard to say on more than one occasion, *'the countryside is my temple and nature is my master'*. I think he was slightly Pagan in leaning, but Sid said that Bill was ex-army and that he didn't think that the army would swear an allegiance to anything that the Queen hadn't a hand in. He wasn't sure whether that included paganism.

Anyway, that aside we'd missed Edna since she'd had a new knee. Edna's husband Harold still joined us and gave us a progress report. She was doing very well, he said, and hoped that she would be back in harness soon. It was all very quick, the whole new knee procedure, in fact, he said, as long as you weren't in pain and could move about ok, you could be home within twenty-four hours of surgery. Edna was one of that lucky group. I knew she had taken a cd of Shakin' Stevens to listen to during the surgery. That was all she needed, she had told me, and as she would be 'screened off from the action' as she put it, she would look on it as rest and recuperation. It's not exactly what I would have called it, but that's our Edna. Harold added that she was doing exercises as directed by the physio' and planned to continue with them even when given the nod to stop. Harold said that Edna had been a real fitness addict in her youth and as she had grown up in Australia, she had always felt a part of the *great outdoors*. I wondered if that was why she coped so well with everything. She was definitely one of life's 'doers'.

Some days I didn't feel a part of the great outdoors at all. Particularly if the walking group went near a lake in a heat wave or at a time of high humidity. I was the one most likely to be nibbled on by the marauding bugs of any size or description. Even the vegetarians of the bug world found something about me to enjoy. I'd mentioned it to Sid, and he said that I should wave elderflowers above my head, that would keep them off. It didn't seem to work; in fact I thought it attracted more than it sent away.

I thought I'd call and visit Edna when we returned from our latest walk, even though I wasn't on the cul de sac visiting rota for the weekend. I was sure she wouldn't mind, and being of Australian heritage I thought she might know a little bit more than Sid did about warding off the undesirables.

Jack Briggs was the walk leader and as I suspected before we left the cafe, this walk would include a water feature somewhere. Jack was like a diviner, he was drawn to the wet stuff. I sighed as we set off and resigned myself to what lay ahead. Sid, who never said much anyway, had very little sympathy.

'For a husband of forty-seven years', I said, 'you don't really understand women.'

Sid silently agreed and we carried on with the walk.

It wasn't long before we reached the high-point of Jack's walk, *Black Knight's Pool,* a local spot of outstanding natural beauty. Of course, Jack was absolutely right; it was a little bit of local paradise. It was also rife with the things that got under my skin, literally. I was bitten to within an inch of my life within five minutes of arrival, and my trouble didn't end there. These blighters didn't mind pastures new; they nibbled at me for every remaining inch of the walk. There would be no release until I was home and in the shower. After that I could dry myself and count the bright, red lumps. After that, out would come the antiseptic cream and cotton wool pads. I knew that within a couple of hours the swelling would arrive, a few hours later, the itching. Walking for health? I wondered whether it was for me. I could walk round the shops, or the cul de sac. I could do lots of things, except it seemed for walking and swimming.

Edna was pleased that I'd decided to call round.

'I'd got you marked on for a Tuesday afternoon visit, after your volunteering stint at the charity shop,' she said.

'This is an extra. I just wondered, you being from Australia and being a fitness fanatic in your youth...'

'Who told you that?'

'Harold. And you still have a little bit of a twang, you can't hide that, so...'

'The twang's there right enough, but I've never been a fitness fanatic. I'm your average Mrs couch potato, like a lot of people.'

'But, when we went swimming, you said you were sorry you wouldn't be able to make it, I thought it was because you were waiting for a new knee.'

'It was, to a degree. I did think I would've enjoyed it. Primrose painted such a wonderful picture, but then when I heard you'd all had to be hoisted out, well I was rather glad that I had an excuse not to join you.'

'But you love the outdoors, you always come with the walking group.'

'Because I don't want to let anyone down. I don't want to be a party pooper.'

'I never would've guessed. Everything you do, you do with so much gusto and enthusiasm.'

I'm a cul de sacer. That's what we do.'

'So, I suppose you won't have any tips that'll help me cope with the random nibbling of flying insects?'

'You could buy a corked hat. That tends to keep them off; they can't do with the swinging of the corks.'

'You mean like the hats they all wear in the outback, in the films?'

'They're the ones.'

'I'll see what I can do.'

It was later than I expected when I returned to the bungalow. Sid had started preparing the evening meal, which was nice. He'd become a bit of a fan of that Heston fellow on tv. I'd watched him too, but he didn't do much for me. I was more of a hairy bikers' girl, (I use the term, *'girl'*, lightly), but at least I didn't have to cook, and it saved Sid from having a conversation; you see Sid, being of the male gender, found it difficult to multi-task, and conversation wasn't his forte either, but to give him his due, he was a very good cook; and it gave me time to myself to make some slight changes to a hat, well not changes exactly, but plans.

I knew there was a safari hat somewhere and I knew that Bill would have a supply of corks.

Tomorrow I would have an Aussie hat. *Jack Briggs*, I thought, *bring on the water feature.*

It was a month before Jack took us near any water, but I was ready. And Edna had joined us for the first time post surgery. She was she said, 'ready for anything'.

I showed her my hat. I was rather impressed with its corks of the champagne variety, whose gleaming metal caught the sun in a dazzling fashion.

'What do you think?' I asked.

'Very good. I've never seen one with champagne corks on before. You've been to Bill's, then?'

'I know. I thought it gave it some extra shuzz.'

I felt on cloud nine as I walked along, corks shaking. Sid didn't walk with me. He said that he had volunteered to be backmarker. I tagged along with Edna and Harold. We were making our way towards another one of Jack's favourite spots, Needham's mill pool. In a way it was one of mine as well. I really liked to see the old mill wheel. It was still in situ even though it didn't move anymore.

I got myself as close as I could to the water's edge. I felt safe in the knowledge that my hat would keep off any unwanted attention from things that fly and bite. Edna smiled. Harold smiled. Sid waved from the back of the group. I waved back so enthusiastically that my wonderful champagne corked hat flew off my head and landed on one of the old paddles of the water wheel. It wasn't going anywhere but I couldn't reach it. A sudden sharpness like the point of a needle piercing my skin was felt on my arm. The back of my neck tingled. My left leg was blotchy.

'Didn't you put on any mossie repellent?' Edna asked.

'I thought I was safe in my hat.'

'Only to a degree,' Edna said.

I looked at Edna. She was in Capri shorts and a tee shirt. Nothing had approached her.

'Have you got the repellent on, then?' I asked.

'Don't need to. They don't go for tough, old Aussie girls like me.'

Bill appeared at the water wheel. 'How are you doing, Rita, thought you'd have had your hat on here?'

There was no point in explaining. It would have seemed like I was a whinger; and in the company of a true Aussie, well you wouldn't get anything from me, and besides, we don't go in for complaining, not in the cul de sac.

7 CHINESE NIGHT

It was while Beattie and I were doing our shift at the charity shop that Julie called in.

Beattie was already a fixture in the shop, but had agreed to do extra hours to cover for Joan, now that she had a foot problem. I was amazed at where Beattie got the energy from. I was glad that Beattie had offered her time as well, though. It meant that I was saved from the brashness of Sylvia, one of the younger volunteers.

We could both see Julie was fit to bursting. 'Have you heard the latest?' Julie said.

I found it difficult to get used to her deep voice, but I don't think I let it show, and the local mixed choir had been quite pleased with her singing ability. The choir, Julie said, 'was another string to her bow'.

Anyway, to get back to where I was, Julie

came into the shop and asked us if we'd heard the latest.

Beattie and I looked at each other. 'Well I certainly haven't heard anything,' I said.

Beattie paused a while, as if in thought, and then said, 'me neither.'

Julie continued, 'I know we don't go in for gossip on the cul de sac, but this isn't the cul de sac, and what I'm about to tell you isn't really gossip, so here goes, 'next door's going to be a Chinese take away.'

'No, really?' I said.

'Positive. There's a sign on the window.'

'Can they do that?' Beattie asked. 'Put a food emporium next to us?'

'We're only a charity shop. I don't think we hold any sway as regards planning applications and approval,' I said.

'Bill would know, maybe we should call an extraordinary meeting of the cul de sac committee tonight,' Julie said.

'I don't think it's anything to do with us. This is the high street, but I suppose we could mention it to Bill in passing. Maybe you should give him a call when you get home.' I said.

'I'm on to it right away,' Julie said. And she left Beattie and me to mull over the bombshell that had just been dropped.

I found out when I returned home that Bill had been straight on to the matter. He'd already contacted the local government department concerned and had been told that it was all going ahead. Apparently there had been notices posted up and down the high street saying that an application had gone in, and they hadn't received any objections.

'There's a meeting at Bill's tonight to further discuss the matter,' Sid said, '20.00 hours prompt.'

'Sounds like Bill's got the bit between his teeth,' I said.

Sid just nodded.

Everyone attended, and Julie was asked to tell us everything she knew, which was pretty much what she'd told me and Beattie in the shop.

'I'd like to ask you, Rita and Beattie, why this has only just been brought to my attention. For goodness sake, ladies, you work right next to where the action's taking place,' Bill said.

'Really Bill, I think you're being rather harsh with the ladies concerned,' Sid said, which really surprised me, but also made me feel quite proud.

Bill continued, 'They're our troops on the ground. Missing something like this is so typical of the way society is going. We all have to be vigilant. I can't stress this enough.'

'If I might speak for me and Beattie, we only volunteer in the charity shop and we're only there for a few hours. The shop next to us has been empty for months. I was only thinking recently, I'll be pleased when it's tenanted again, particularly as it's coming towards winter and the nights are drawing in. I think we ladies like to know we've a neighbour at hand in case of a problem.'

'Yes, 'I can understand that,' Bill said, 'But I wished you'd noticed earlier. Take away premises are notorious for attracting the wrong type of person, and then there's the litter issue. Are there enough bins? And then there are rats; where there's litter the rats aren't very far behind.'

'I don't think it'll be that bad,' Primrose said, 'and a take away might be handy, if you're back late anytime, or don't feel like cooking. Let's at least give the venture a chance, that's what I say.'

'The voice of youth,' Bill replied, and then added, 'Well Julie, you were the one who raised the issue, what do you want to do?'

'I only mentioned it because I thought you might be interested in what's going on in the town. I didn't want to cause bother or anything.'

'Did you get a name or an address for the new proprietor?' Bill asked.

'Not the name of the proprietor, no; but I know what it's going to be called. It's going to be called, The Tan Lan Fryer.'

'I must say, not a very imaginative name, is it?' Bill said, and then continued, 'Right, all that remains for me to do is to bring the meeting to a close. Anything you hear, for or against the venture, let me know. You never know when such information may come in useful.'

I was glad to get back home. I really like Bill, and he does wonders for the cul de sac, but tonight, tonight I felt like I was back at school and on report to the headmaster. I think Sid noticed. He went and made me a cup of tea.

The next few weeks passed and there was a lot of coming and going at the new take away. Beattie and I watched from the charity shop, when we weren't busy of course. Sylvia, the volunteer who liked to make her presence felt, had surprisingly, suddenly announced that she had been informed by Head Office that she could act as manageress in Muriel's absence; (Muriel having had to take leave at short notice to deal with an elderly mother with a broken hip.) This was all news to Beattie and myself, of course. Muriel had said nothing to us, and neither had Head Office for that matter.

We didn't let it bother us, of course. When you live in a cul de sac you have to get along with people at close quarters. You develop 'broad shoulders' so there was nothing that Sylvia could say that would cause us to take offence. Even when Sylvia asked us what was so interesting about the re-fit at the shop next door, because to be perfectly honest, the answer was there was nothing really interesting about it, it was just a diversion, I suppose.

The men there worked really hard, and despite information received, there was a noticeable lack of anyone oriental. They, whoever 'they' were, were having a lovely new counter fitted and the tiling was quite exquisite. It was something I would have quite happily had in my own kitchen, and I'm not the least bit oriental. It rather surprised me, actually. I mentioned it to Sid when I arrived home.

I said to him that I might have to start doing my family tree. He couldn't see the point of it. He said words to the effect of, *he was here, he knew who he was and that was all there was to it,* which I suppose ought to be enough for anyone.

Later that week, Julie asked me if I'd anything to report back, or whether there was anything she ought to pass on to Bill. I told her about the exquisite tiling, but she didn't think that was relevant. The next Tuesday though, there was something to report. When Beattie and I turned up at the charity shop, Sylvia was waiting for us.

'Girls, I've got some fab news. The Tan Lan Fryery opens on Saturday, there's a notice in the window.'

'They've soon got the work finished, haven't they?' I said.

'It doesn't take these shopfitters long once they've got a good run at it, and the place is empty.'

'Have you noticed the staff? What do they look like?' I said.

'I don't know,' Sylvia replied, 'I've only seen the sign in the window. Anyway, the reason I'm mentioning it at all is that Muriel's been in, her mother's quite on the way to recovery now, and she's left her in the safe hands of the, 'Meadow Rise', care home. Her mother will be there for another fortnight. Anyway, Muriel's seen the shop and she's offered to buy us a meal from next door when they open. Can you ladies be here at lunch time, Saturday?'

'I suppose so,' I said.

Beattie said she could manage it, but wasn't sure that she liked Chinese food. In fact she said it would be a first because she'd never had Chinese food but she was willing to try it.

Sylvia said, 'That's great. I'll give Muriel a call and let her know.'

She disappeared into the back office.

'I hope I can cope with Chinese,' Beattie said.

'Of course you'll be able to cope with a Chinese. You live in a cul de sac.'

When I arrived home I was full of it I can tell you. Sid didn't say much, so I don't exactly know what he thought of me going for a meal from work.

I got out my recipe books. I found one that I'd won in a Christmas raffle at a local charity event. It was called, *'Cooking Chinese-style'*, which I thought was as close as you could possibly get to Chinese food without being authentic. Nothing jumped out at me. I thought I might cook something before Saturday, so I wouldn't be a, 'Chinese food virgin', as it were. There seemed to be a lot of noodles needed and something called Hoisin sauce; plums featured greatly as well. I opened my kitchen cupboards and had a look, nothing remotely Chinese so I improvised. I made us spaghetti on toast for tea, followed by prunes and custard. Sid thought it a strange mix, but I told him it was Chinese-style, and that I was preparing myself for Saturday.

'Do we have to have it again on Saturday?'

he asked.

'No, you don't, but I'm having lunch with friends from the charity shop. We're going to the new Chinese, this is a run through.'

Sid just nodded.

On Saturday, Beattie and I walked to the charity shop in time for the grand opening of The Tan Lan Fryery.

'This is really exciting,' Beattie said, 'I think I've told you we've not eaten Chinese food before.'

'You did, Beattie.'

'And what about you, do you like Chinese?'

'I have to confess, I'm not au fait with a lot of their dishes but I like to ring the changes, so Sid and I ate semi-Chinese on Tuesday. We're quite cosmopolitan in that respect.'

'What respect's that?' Beattie asked.

'In respect of the food. We eat a variety of foods, from different countries.'

'Ray doesn't like a lot of foreign food,' Beattie said, 'In fact sometimes he pulls his face at Welsh rarebit.'

'Why don't you call it cheese on toast, he'd probably eat it then.'

'He doesn't like cheese,' Beattie replied.

The take away was swathed in bunting, and the smells coming from the establishment didn't smell very foreign; in fact it smelled like good old fish and chips.

'This is just like being at the sea-side, this

is,' I said.

We went into the charity shop. Sylvia and Muriel were there.

'Oh good, ladies, you've arrived. We've got the kettle on in the back, so what would you like, here have a look at the menu,' Muriel said.

I took the menu and Beattie and I studied it.

'This is an English menu,' Beattie said.

'Yes, I thought it was going to be a Chinese. I was looking for a different eating experience,' I said.

'I'm sorry to disappoint you Rita, but it's chips with either fish, pudding or pie, maybe a sausage if you're lucky. And where did you get the idea that it was going to be a Chinese take away?' Muriel asked.

'It was my neighbour, Julie. She said it was going to be called, 'The Tan Lan Fryery.'

'And it is. Tan Lan's in Wales. Rob, the owner, is from there. He felt it had a certain ring to it, just right for a traditional fish and chip shop. You could say that he's gone back to his roots, in a roundabout way. It's fitted out lovely, it really is, and he's some lovely pictures on the wall. I bet Sid and Ray would like to go and have a look at the pictures, they're of the old railway line through Mostyn. And you know how men love trains,' Muriel said.

I didn't know whether Sid liked trains or not. I'd never thought to ask him.

'So no noodles or plums or hoisin sauce?' I asked.

'Definitely not,' Muriel said.

'In that case I'll have cod and chips.'

Beattie waited a moment and then said, 'I'm going to enjoy this, no frying, no washing-up and all the fish bits I can eat, did you get that Muriel? That's the same as Rita but with fish bits, and lots of vinegar.'

'You two are easy to please. Sylvia, brew the tea and I'll be back in a tick, and get out the best china, we've got some Braganza plates in the back that haven't sold. Fish and chips tastes better off a china plate,' then she paused and added, 'I've got the best volunteers in the business, it's surprising what you can learn from ladies who live in a cul de sac.'

8 POPPY ALWAYS RINGS TWICE

The only time we've ever had any unpleasantness in the cul de sac, (Bill's car/cd episode aside,) was when Poppy Sutcliffe arrived. And the funny thing was, she wasn't from the cul de sac, no, she was from one of the adjacent through roads. As you can imagine, the first time I made her acquaintance I was fraught, left reeling if the truth be known, but that was only the beginning.

I'd seen her from the lounge window, I didn't know who she was then, mind; we hadn't been introduced. Anyway she came into the cul de sac and marched up to our bungalow, opened the gate and marched up the path and rang the door bell, TWICE. Well, as you can imagine, from that moment I was on my guard. No one in the cul de sac rings another's bell twice, not without waiting for a decent interval, and I can assure you no interval of any sort was given. It was just two rings, one after the other. Almost a continuous ring. So, prepared, I went and answered the door. I was on my own. Sid had nipped off to help at the allotment. The allotment was another of Bill's initiatives and I must admit it was another good one. Everyone dibbed in for the rent of the plot and seeds etc, and then the produce; veg, fruit, flowers, were shared out between us. We ladies of the cul de sac loved it. And the potatoes were something else. You've got to hand it to Bill. He's really good at what he does. He's a one man powerhouse. No wonder he was in the army.

Anyway, to get back to Poppy; I answered the door and saw her standing there.

'Hello,' she said, 'I've just moved on to Moonshine Avenue, it's only around the corner.'

I didn't know where any of this was leading. I just stood and looked at her. She paused, looked back at me and said, 'Do you know it?'

'Yes', I replied.

'Perhaps I should introduce myself, I'm Poppy Sutcliffe. My husband, John, has recently retired so we've downsized.'

'Oh,' I said.

'Yes, we're new to the area. It's very nice, isn't it?'

'Yes,' I replied.

'I wanted to ask you something.'

'Ask away,' I said; still no nearer knowing where any of this was leading.

'I feel a bit cheeky really, we only moved in on Saturday.'

'Oh,' I said, 'Was that you? I thought I noticed a van. The weather was with you at any rate. There's nothing worse than a wet removal day.'

'Quite.'

I stood and looked at Poppy. 'You haven't asked me anything yet,' I said.

'No, no you see I play Mah Jong. I've heard from a neighbour that in the cul de sac you play on a Monday afternoon. I'd like to join the club.'

'It isn't a club. We're just friends who live in the cul de sac and who meet up to play.'

'But you have a league. You play for the 'Magic Pagoda.'

'Where did you hear that?'

'I'd rather not say.'

'Well I'm sorry, Poppy. We don't need anyone else in our group and you really do have to live in the cul de sac to be invited.'

'But I'm less than five minutes away. I literally join on to the cul de sac.'

'I'm sorry Poppy, that's the way it is. Now, if you don't mind, I really have to go.'

I knew I'd have to wait until the men returned from the allotment. Bill would have to hear of this. I felt a panic attack coming on, something that's unheard of in the cul de sac. I made myself some peppermint tea and 'phoned Beattie.

Right away, as soon as I'd explained, Beattie was on my side.

'Oh no, Rita, we can't have that. You've done the right thing, telling her no.'

'You think so?'

'Of course, and you're right about getting

Bill involved. That's always the best thing to do; pass any unsavoury business on to the head honcho.'

As soon as Bill was available I told him what had happened. He wasn't very pleased, I can tell you.

'Does anyone else know about it?'

'I mentioned it to Sid, and of course I've told Beattie, and you Bill, that's it.'

'Good, don't say anything else. We'll try and keep it under our hat. I feel this is like a loaded gun. It could go off at any time.'

'Oh, I see. But, as regards keeping it to ourselves, well I daresay Beattie will have mentioned it to Ray by now.'

'Yes, yes, thank you for pointing that out, well as long as it doesn't go beyond the cul de sac.'

'I understand Bill. My lips are sealed.'

Even having mentioned things to Bill, I was still nervous the next time we were at Frank and Julie's for the afternoon's Mah Jong. I kept jumping at the slightest noise, wondering what would happen, wondering when the loaded gun might go off. Every time the sparrows twittered I imagined the click of a revolver. It didn't happen.

After a few weeks I finally calmed down. The palpitations were less and I was drinking fewer cups of peppermint tea.

It was Monday. The cul de sac afternoon for Mah Jong. Sid and I were the hosts. Everything was ready; the draw had been made and the nibbles were strategically placed. That was when it happened; two rings on the door bell. As soon as I heard it I knew.

'It's Poppy Sutcliffe,' I said.

'Can you be sure?' Bill asked.

'I'd know her ring anywhere,' I said.

'Do you mind if I go to the door?' Bill asked.

'Please do,' I said, breathing a sigh of relief that the ball had been taken out of my court.

'What do you think she wants?' Edna asked.

'She wants to play Mah Jong,' I said.

'But she can't,' Edna replied. 'She's not one of the group.'

'Try telling her that,' I said.

Bill returned; Poppy following close behind like a lap dog. I could see that she'd been crying. What could Bill have said to her?

'You'd better sit down, over there on the settee,' Bill said to Poppy.

'Rita, would you make Poppy a cup of strong, sweet tea? She's had rather a shock.' He looked at Poppy. 'Are you all right, my dear?' Bill asked.

I went into the kitchen. Beattie followed after me, she asked, 'Do you think that Poppy and Bill are previously acquainted?

'I don't know what's going on, Beattie. But he did call her 'my dear' and she had been crying.'

Beattie went back into the lounge. I followed on with a tea-tray and cups, enough for everybody. I poured a cup and handed it to Poppy.

'Thank you, Rita,' she said. 'It's so kind of you.'

Bill stood up. 'I think we'd better call off this afternoon's session,' he said.

I looked around the room. Everyone had a slightly bemused expression on their face.

'I'll put the tiles away then, if that's it,' I said.

'I think that would be the best under the circumstances.'

Poppy began to cry. I passed her a box of tissues. She smiled at me. Bill looked at her.

'Shall I tell them, my dear?'

'Would you?'

Bill continued. 'Poppy's had some very distressing news. As you all know, she and her husband, John, moved into the area a couple of months ago. Well, John was taken into hospital last night, a suspected heart attack. Then just before eleven o'clock this morning the hospital rang. They asked Poppy to get there as soon as possible. She was with John when he died'.

A hush came over the room. We didn't really know Poppy at all but it was still a shock.

Bill spoke again, 'Poppy knows no one here. All her family are in the south of England. Her son and his family will be coming up tomorrow, but Poppy hasn't really made any friends in the area, and none of her neighbours were in. She had to tell someone about it, and she thought of us, realised that we'd all be at Mah Jong today; so she watched to see where we were going, whose house we would be meeting in, and then she came across. Poppy knew that she would find some support in the cul de sac; now, doesn't that make you proud, eh?'

I don't know about proud, I was lost for words. I couldn't think of anything to say, and Sid, well, you know him; he's not likely to say much at the best of times, so he was exceptionally quiet, given what had happened.

We all just sat, let Poppy talk if she wanted. It was like that for the best part of an hour. Poppy said she was glad of the company; that was all that she wanted.

When it approached five o'clock, people started to drift away home. It had been a strange afternoon.

Bill, ever the true gentleman, escorted Poppy home. He linked her arm in his, and saw her to her door. I watched from the window. He didn't go in.

9 A CUL DE SAC AFFAIR, PART ONE, AGONY

When Beattie and I turned up for our stint at the charity shop one Tuesday, we found Rob deep in conversation with Sylvia. It was just after the opening of the *'Tan Lan Fryery'*.

Rob, the owner of the *Tan Lan,* (as we called it), had taken to coming in and asking Sylvia for advice. The subjects he wanted advice on were many and varied. One day it would be growing roses and dealing with greenfly, the next it would be how long tea needs to brew, properly; or what to buy his mother for her birthday. Now why he should think Sylvia would be able to furnish answers to any of those questions, I don't know. I said right away, as soon as I heard him asking Sylvia that very first time, I said, 'She's too young to know these things, (Sylvia's difficult to age, but I can tell she's not much more than a girl, perhaps mid-twenties, and in my book, that's a girl.) I said to Rob, 'Beattie would know the answers to all of your questions.'

Rob didn't pay any attention to me and carried on talking to Sylvia.

I mentioned to Muriel that Rob was spending a lot of time talking to Sylvia. Jokingly I said, 'What he needs is an agony aunt.'

'What a great idea,' Muriel said. 'We'll try it in the shop. People always have problems that a stranger can solve.'

'But we know everyone, we're not strangers.'

'Leave it with me,' Muriel said, 'I'll think of something.'

And she did. A few weeks later and Muriel came in with a box where people seeking help could post their problems, anonymously. 'They would,' she said, 'call in later in the day and collect the answer to their problem.'

'Who's going to answer the problems?' I asked.

'You and Beattie, who else?'

'But will we have enough time? We have the shop to see to?'

'Sylvia can serve while you spend half an hour answering as many queries as you can.'

'Are people paying for this service?' I asked.

'Of course. We're a charity shop, people can leave a donation.'

Muriel seemed to have it all sorted out. I wasn't so sure.

The next Tuesday there was a notice in the window. *Tuesdays only. Have your problems solved by our dedicated team. The answers to all your questions from gardening to romance. (A small donation required)*

'Muriel's been on the ball,' I said.

'I wish she hadn't,' Beattie replied.

'Don't worry about it. I'm sure we'll cope, and in a way you know, you remind me of Marje Proops.'

'She's dead.'

'Well that doesn't matter. She wore big glasses and answered problems. She had a column in the *Daily Mirror* for years,' I said. 'It was called, *Dear Marje.*'

Beattie just looked at me.

'Ladies, ladies,' Muriel said as we walked into the shop, 'you'll not believe this, we've some problems for the agony aunts already. You two go through to the office and get comfy. I'll bring the papers through. You'll have to keep the questions together with the relevant answers when you've replied, of course; we don't want them to get separated and give someone a wrong solution.'

'No', I replied. Truth be told, I felt a bit shaky. What if people twigged that the agony aunts were me and Beattie?

'Here you are. There are four for you to get on with,' Muriel said.

'Will Sylvia be able to cope in the shop, on

her own?'

'She'll be fine. I can always pop out of the office if needs be, now come along, these people will all be calling back for their replies this afternoon. Chop, chop!'

Beattie unfolded the first paper and began to read, *'I've recently moved into the area and am finding it difficult to make friends'.*

'That's easy, they should join local groups and organisations initially, and then take it from there.'

'Oh, very good Beattie, next one please.'

'Here we are, *'my wife doesn't understand me, we seem to be drifting apart'.* What do you think, Rita? This sounds a toughie.'

'I think we should say something like, *'try and understand your wife, talk to her more, don't allow yourself to drift, think back to when you first met and try and relive some of those early memories'.'*

'I'm enjoying this, Rita. I really am.'

'Me too. It makes a change from being in the shop all the time.'

'It certainly does. Right, next one, oh Rita, this is easy, *'what would bring a grass stain out of my son's cricket whites?'*

'It might be easy for you Beattie, but I've no idea. I'm afraid you're on your own with this one.'

'Ray used to play when he was younger. It was something you had to do every week in the season. You just have to rub the stained area with a cloth soaked in white vinegar, leave it for ten to fifteen minutes and then rinse in cold water and wash as normal.'

'Does it work?'

'Not all the time. I think it depends on how long the stain has been left, but it usually looks better.'

'I think we should include a warning with this one. We don't want to have to be forking out for cricket whites, do we?'

'No, I think you're very sensible Rita. I'll put a note on the end of the reply; belt and braces approach is always best.'

'When you've done that, you can read the last problem out.'

'Won't be a tick. Right, here we are. *'Do you know any quick ways of cleaning silver?'* What would you suggest, Rita, sudsy water and then dry in a towel?'

'Either that or a proprietary silver dip, that's what I use.'

'I'll write them both down, that's it, finished.'

We went back into the shop, Muriel said that there'd been £10.68p left in the donations box. We thought it was quite good for the few minutes it had taken.

'You'll do it again, next week, ladies?'

'Of course,' we replied.

And we did. The charity shop agony aunts were receiving wide local acclaim. We had a reputation for giving straightforward, no-nonsense answers, and I enjoyed it, I really did. It gave a new vitality to our Tuesday volunteering stints.

Rob was still coming in talking to Sylvia. It was more of a chat they indulged in now. He didn't seem to ask for answers to problems anymore. Sometimes I thought that he was spending more time in the charity shop chatting with Sylvia than he was in his own establishment. Occasionally he'd fetch Beattie and me some fish and chips, so I decided it was better not to notice just how much time he was spending chatting with Sylvia. The fish and chips from the Tan Lan were delicious. Rob's shop was one of the best things to happen in our town for a long time. And Muriel didn't mind us eating at the premises, not as long as we stayed in the back.

We'd been doing the resolving of people's problems for about six weeks when we received a rather strange request. Beattie's jaw dropped as she read; *'I've fallen for a lady, recently widowed. How long do you think is a decent interval before I make a move?'* Are you thinking what I'm thinking?' Beattie asked.

'Do you mean you think that it could be Bill and Poppy?'

'Exactly,' she said.

'Then we'll have to tread carefully, leave it to one side, we'll answer the others first and then come back to that one.'

'Good idea, right, this one says, *'I play Mah Jong with a group of friends, but now find I can play online, shall I leave the group?'*

Beattie looked at me, 'It's like all the cul de sac is in our post bag. What do you think it means?'

'I don't know yet, read another.'

Beattie began, *'I recently married a much younger woman, she spends a lot of her time on the internet...'* Beattie paused, 'this could be Brian and Primrose. Poor Brian is worried about losing Primrose.'

'Well if our post bag is anything to go by she's only playing Mah Jong; he's nothing to worry about.'

'I don't like this Rita. Everything is beginning to sound too close to home. It's as though we've opened a Pandora's box. I'm not sure I can carry on with this anymore. We'll have to tell Muriel and she'll be upset, there'll be donations in the box.'

'Yes, she'll be upset, but what else can we do? Oh, and by the way, it mightn't all be bad'

'What do you mean by that?'.

'At the bottom of Pandora's box, hope remained.'

'Is that supposed to cheer me up?' Beattie asked.

'I don't know, either way, let's go and break the news to Muriel.

As we thought, Muriel wasn't pleased, not at all. She said that we couldn't just stop. We had to answer the problems as though there was no connection to us, which, she said, there probably wasn't. She said that it was known in the cul de sac that we worked in the charity shop, so why should anyone from the cul de sac come in and ask for advice?

She was right of course. We just hadn't thought it through.

The next Tuesday when we arrived at the shop, Muriel asked us to go straight through to her office. Sylvia smiled at us both in a way that only a young person can. We knew straight away that there was a problem. When we were in the office, Muriel closed the door behind us and asked us to have a seat.

'What were you two thinking of last week? I knew you had reservations about the problems posed, but I thought we'd got over that.'

I looked at Beattie. 'You tell Muriel,' she said.

'Well Rita? Muriel said.

'We decided to cover all bases.'

'Carry on,' Muriel said.

'We answered as though they were the people in the cul de sac, as though they were the people we knew.'

'And that's it?'

'That's it,' I said.

'Well it mustn't happen again. I've just had a very upset elderly gentleman in here. He's been 'walking out' with a lady for two years; she was widowed like him, and after twelve months they went to a tea dance together. That was two years ago and now he'd like to make it more permanent. He wants to marry the lady. He was rather upset that he was advised a wait of five years would be appropriate...'

'I'm sorry,' I said, 'but Beattie and I thought

it was someone we knew. The lady in question has only just lost her husband, we thought for her it would be too soon.'

'But it wasn't her,' Muriel said, 'And if this gentleman tells others, which he might, our service will have to come to an end, and that would be sad, because up to now you've been very successful. Over the past few weeks of the scheme it's raised a little over five hundred pounds in donations to our charity.

Beattie and I gasped. We were amazed.

'Well ladies, what do you think, are you going to carry on providing answers for the good people of our town, and are you going to answer them appropriately, not go off down any made up cul de sacs?'

I looked at Beattie. 'What do you think?'

'I don't know. I think it was enjoyable when it started, but I'm beginning to feel under pressure.'

'Me too,' I said.

Muriel called through to Sylvia, 'Put closed on the shop door and come through to the office.'

A few minutes later Sylvia joined us.

'Sylvia, could you make us all a cup of tea and bring it in here please, and tea for yourself, of course.'

'Ok', she replied, 'is there a problem?'

'Nothing that we can't sort out,' Muriel said.

Sylvia returned about ten minutes later and she poured us all a drink. Muriel spoke first.

'I think Rita and Beattie are finding the problem post bag stressful. Do you think you could take over, Sylvia?'

'Sylvia looked quite surprised. 'I don't know. I think it needs someone with plenty of life experience. I think that means an older person,' she said.

'Thanks for the young vote,' Muriel said, 'Any questions, ladies?'

'You still want us to be the agony aunts, then? I said.

'If you'd like to carry on, yes.'

'We could give it another month or two, and then see where we are. I don't know if I'll be carrying on in to the New Year anyway,' Beattie said.

'You mean you're giving up the charity shop work, what will Bill say?' I said, 'You know how keen he is on the 'big society' idea. He's not going to like it.'

'But it's what I want Rita. I'm getting too old for all this, and I think this will be my last winter as a volunteer.'

'We've certainly opened up something now,' Muriel said, 'But I suppose it's as you were for the time being.'

'As you were's exactly it,' I said.

And it was, for the time being. I just couldn't believe what I was hearing from Beattie. I wondered what had brought about this change of heart.

I mentioned everything to Sid when I arrived home, as usual he'd nothing much to say, but I suppose he was a good listener, and that was what I wanted at the moment.

Over the next few weeks I tried to coax Beattie into telling me her reasons. She was being very secretive about everything, and as we were such good friends, I felt as though I was being cut out. It was difficult to understand and I knew I couldn't push Beattie into telling me; that would be prying, and we don't like to pry, not in the cul de sac.

Beattie had started to call round for me when it was our Tuesday at the charity shop and we'd walk into town together. This walk was when we'd talk and discuss things, but lately Beattie had become very tight-lipped. I knew there was something the matter, but how to get to the bottom of it, that was my problem.

We answered the problems that Muriel had set aside for us. There were only two. I said to Beattie, 'Probably dropping off as it's getting nearer to Christmas. Everybody wants to be happy at Christmas, don't they?'

Beattie set off crying. 'I'm not happy at all,' she said.

'I knew there was something,' I said, 'But thought it was just pressure of work, and I didn't want you to feel that I was busy-bodying.'

'I wish you had been more pushy. I've wanted to tell you about it for weeks but I couldn't bring myself to, and, and it's terrible.'

'Nothing can be that bad, nothing. Now are you going to tell me?'

'It's Ray. He's having an affair, I know he

is.'

'No, not your Ray. I'm sure this has to be a terrible mistake. Your Ray would never do anything of the kind, he's not the type.'

'That's where they've got you. They're all the type, if they're tempted.'

'Is that why you're thinking of giving up working in the shop?'

'Partly.'

'What do you mean, 'partly'?'

'Well, partly. Partly Ray and partly because I'm beginning to feel my age, and you see Ray's younger than me; so I assume he wants a younger model. He thinks I'm past it.'

'Has he given you any reason to believe all this?'

'He's started singing in the shower.'

'Is that it?'

'Well, that and he's started using, 'Colour Me for Men' on his hair. His hair's darker now than when we got married.'

'If that's all you're basing your worries on, you've nothing to worry about Beattie. Men do more than that when they're having an affair. They go off for the evening without a reasonable excuse. They return smelling of cheap scent and they start keep fit.'

'How do you know all this?'

'My mother told me, although why if someone's having an affair they can't afford decent perfume, I've never really understood.'

'Do you think it's all a waste of time, Rita? It's driving me crazy, I'm losing sleep.'

'You need to pull yourself together, Beattie. I'm sure there's nothing going on.'

'It was Poppy who sowed the seed of doubt in my mind, when she called round a few weeks ago.'

'Ah, we're getting somewhere now,' I said, 'What did she do?'

'She came round to borrow some loppers for the apple tree, and Ray went back with her. They were gone for quite a long time, and when he came back he was flushed, and since then he's been doing the other things, the singing and Colour Me for Men.'

'I might have known she'd be at the bottom of it, but the only chap she has time for is Bill. You mark my words, there's something going on there, and it's not origami. You must have heard how Bill called her, *'my dear'.*'

'Yes, but that was weeks ago. She's moved on to my Ray now, I'm sure of it.'

'No, trust me Beattie, she's not moved anywhere.'

Beattie smiled but I could see that she wasn't convinced.

When we came back into the shop, Muriel said, You've been gone a long time. There were only two problems.'

'Yes', I said, 'but they were very complex.'

'Right, I'll get back to my office then, and when Sylvia comes back, tell her I want a quick word.'

'Where is she?' I asked.

'She's popped into the Tan Lan to see Rob.'

'She's seeing a lot of him, lately,' I said.

'Too much, I sometimes think,' Muriel replied.

Christmas was getting ever nearer. And as the weeks went on Beattie seemed slightly better, re Ray. She told me that she'd wait until the holiday was over before she started making plans about what to do in the shop and what to do about Ray. She had a lot to consider, she said. I told her that I'd have a word with Bill. I was sure that he held the key to Beattie's problems. I waited for her to tell me 'no, don't do that'. But she didn't.

I mentioned to Sid that I had to pop round to Bill's, that Beattie had a problem. He didn't bat an eyelid, which wasn't unusual, and I went on my way.

When I returned, I don't even think he'd noticed that I'd gone in the first place. He was asleep, paper in lap. I went into the kitchen and started to prepare the meal, hoping the aroma of something cooking would bring Sid gently back to the land of the living. Hot-pot with a suet crust was one of his favourites, and it didn't fail. He glanced at the clock as I came through with the plates, 'It's got late,' he said.

'Thought I'd leave you while you were sleeping. You looked contented,' I said.

He always did look contented when he was sleeping. I think it was to do with the fact that he had now lost most of his hair. It gave him the appearance of a big baby.

The hot-pot was good. I think it was a case of me being ready for it, as well. It had been a hectic day, but it finished with a good feeling as I thought I'd managed to sort out a problem that was bothering a good friend. I couldn't say anything to Beattie, not yet, but eventually all would be revealed.

The next time we went down to the charity shop I could tell Beattie was feeling better, she looked in brighter spirit. I couldn't help myself,

'What's happened, you seem more like your old self,' I said.

'I think you might have been right about Ray.

'How's that?' I asked.

'He's stopped using any type of toiletry on his hair and the singing's almost stopped as well.'

'And that's better?'

'Yes, I'm sure it is.'

I knew it was, but I couldn't say anything, my lips were sealed.

Sylvia should have been in the shop when we arrived, but she hadn't turned up. Muriel was in quite a flap. 'But she doesn't come in until lunch time, she's not late yet,' I said.

'She is,' Muriel replied. 'Betty 'phoned in sick last night and I left a message on Sylvia's answer-phone for her to come in at ten this morning. She's not here, is she? Anyway, as soon as you two ladies are in situ, I'll call her on her mobile, see what she's up to.'

'Strange don't you think, Sylvia not turning up, and not a word?'
Beattie smiled. 'Oh Rita, how could you have missed that one, and you an agony aunt?'

'Beattie, you don't usually beat around any kind of bush, so please could you get to the point. I've no idea what you're talking about.'

'Sylvia and Rob from the *Tan Lan,* they're an 'item'. I believe that's the latest jargon for folk who are, as we used to say, 'courting'.'

'You mean...'

'Yes. It was obvious from the start, the way he kept coming in and asking for 'advice'.'

'I never thought for a moment...'

'No, I know, but I did.'

Muriel came out of the office to find Beattie and me laughing, not loudly you understand, but quietly, after all, we were in public, even though there was no one in the shop.

'What's all that about?' Muriel asked.

'Beattie's just mentioned that there's something going on between Rob and Sylvia. She's surprised that I missed it.'

'You and me both,' Muriel said. 'I've just managed to get in touch with Sylvia. She's in Paris with Rob; they're married.'

'Married,' Beattie and I said together.

'Yes, married', Muriel said, 'and if that's not enough she won't be coming back. She's going to be helping Rob out at the Tan Lan Fryer. I shall have to advertise, and it'll be difficult getting someone, particularly at this time of year.'

The card stand by the door moved and Poppy appeared.

'Pardon me for over-hearing, but I can help,' she announced.

'Muriel smiled. 'And who are you?' she asked.

'Poppy. Poppy Sutcliffe'.

I watched Beattie's face as it changed, from relaxed and happy, to pale and fraught. I'd spoken to Bill; he said that he'd everything in hand. This wasn't supposed to happen. Bill never mentioned that Poppy would volunteer for the shop.

I looked across at Muriel. Her face told a different story. She was as pleased as anything.

'Come with me Poppy, and we'll interview you now, if you like,' she said.

When the two of them came out of the office they were both laughing and chatting like old friends. Muriel showed Poppy to the door and then came over to us.

'She's a lovely lady. New to the area. And you'd never guess it to look at her but she's only recently widowed. Anyway, she's going to give us a try next week. She'll do the same hours that Sylvia did and we'll take it from there, but for the time being at least, we're sorted.'

Muriel walked back to her office and was obviously pleased as punch with the outcome. I just hoped that Beattie and I managed to make it to Christmas at the charity shop, but for now, there was nothing I could do or say about anything.

10 A CUL DE SAC AFFAIR, PART TWO, THE BIG SING

I think all of us in the cul de sac enjoyed Christmas. Our big charity fundraiser of the season was *The Big Sing.* We all got together, under Bill's supervision of course, and practised all the seasonal favourites; Christmas carols and lots of Christmas songs. *White Christmas* was a perennial choice. I think we all enjoyed singing that one. And who wouldn't warm to the strains of *The Christmas Song?* I don't know whether people thought of Nat King Cole when they heard us, but they all seemed to enjoy it anyway. And then there were the children's favourites, *Frosty the Snowman* and *Rudolf the Red Nosed Reindeer*; adults joined in with these as well, it must be said.

We would sing to raise money for a local charity or cause. When we met at Bill's we all threw names into the hat, as it were, and then had a vote. The winner was that year's chosen charity.

Then of course we had to choose the song list. That first meeting at Bill's was a mammoth task, but it was also a lot of fun.

It was decided that this year's Big Sing would raise money for the local *Riding for the Disabled.* Primrose had been a keen rider as a girl and she said that anyone could get a boost from riding, and then she said there was the connection made between the horse and rider. This she said, *'must never be dismissed. It's a vital part of the experience.'*

Primrose also used a lot of words like, 'connection' and 'bonding'. I think it was because she was still in paid work. Her recent marriage to Brian had given him a new lease of life. He was like a teenager again. His words, not mine; but good luck to him, that's what I say.

Anyway, Primrose used a lot of these words and by and large we all knew what she meant, by and large. Gladys maintained that she was *up to speed* as she worked on reception for the local vet, Mr McGluskey.

I don't know how *au fait* Gladys was with a lot of things but one thing I did know, I didn't appreciate it when either Primrose or Gladys mentioned *thinking out of the box* or *blue sky thinking.* It left me cold, but I never let it show. You see we don't do that sort of thing, not in the cul de sac. It would be thought of as rude, and rudeness of any kind just isn't tolerated. I suppose Primrose would say that we're *inclusive.*

Right, to get back to the Big Sing, we'd

been to Bill's, sorted out the song list and the charity and arranged the evenings for practise. As Primrose put it, *'we'd broken the back of the organisational monster.*

'Yes,' Bill said, 'I'm going to contact Dean and Fraser, see if we can sing in their foyer again. When I've done that, I'll let everyone have a list of dates; if possible by the end of next week. So remember folks, keep those diaries free.'

Beattie and I went to put the kettle on; we felt as though we'd earned it.

The next week, and as promised, Bill had finalised the dates. As usual Dean and Fraser were accommodating. Everything was going to plan. The dates for singing were Wednesday, Thursday and Friday evening in the run up to Christmas, and our usual 'Big Sing Extravaganza' on the Saturday afternoon. Before the afternoon extravaganza the men drew lots to see who would be dressing up as Father Christmas to lead the bucket collection. They pulled their faces a little at this, but I think they all enjoyed it. We were under way!

The first rehearsal would be at Bill's the following Friday evening, between seven and nine o'clock.

After the final sing of the weekend, that was when we all went to Bill's for a celebratory drink, champagne of course, and totted up the final total. We liked to get to the thousand pound mark, and most years we did.

We'd been going to Bill's for rehearsals for

about three weeks. Well there was no *about it,* at all; it was exactly three weeks. That was when Bill surprised us all. He stood there, in front of us all, in his conservatory and said, 'I'd like another person to join in the singing.'

We all looked at one another, and then back at Bill. He carried on. 'There's a problem with it, but I'd like your approval.'

'What's the problem?' I asked.

'This person is not from the cul de sac, and this person has a particularly fine contralto voice.'

'Do we know her?' Primrose asked.

'I'm not sure about everyone, but I think most of you have seen her. She's recently been bereaved.'

'It can't be, is it Poppy?' I asked.

'Yes,' Bill replied, 'I'd like your approval and then she could join us next week. She is an excellent singer, thought about turning professional when she was younger.'

Beattie nudged me and was just about to speak when Bill said, 'Now Beattie, anything you have to say, you can say it to all of us.'

'I was just thinking, you must be quite pally as you've heard her sing and know a little about her past.'

'Quite right Beattie. We are firm friends. We became so after John died. I've been helping her to cope with her bereavement.'

Beattie glanced at me and smiled. I knew she would be mightily relieved. Then she looked across at Ray, and winked.

I sighed. It was a relief for me as well. I'd

been keeping this news close to my chest for weeks. I must admit though, the way everything had all come out did seem rather odd, and Poppy was still volunteering in the charity shop. Muriel had informed me and Beattie that Poppy took to everything like a duck to water. Neither of us was surprised.

The room was quiet for a few minutes and then Frank spoke,

'The cul de sac seems to me to be a 'we all help one another democracy'; rather like our PM's 'big society' that you often speak of Bill, but on a smaller scale, of course, so in the way of a democracy why don't we all have a vote on it?'

There was another silence, and then Bill said, 'If that's what you want.'

The following Friday Poppy was already at Bill's when we arrived. She had a bit of a sheepish look about her. I assumed she hadn't just arrived, but had been there for some time. Anyway, Bill was right about one thing, her voice. It was beautiful, and it did add a lot to our singing of *Good King Wenceslas* and *Joy to the World*.

I didn't let anything slip by me this time. From the way Bill and Poppy were behaving, I would say they were an 'item'. What was that line in the song, *when love walks in and takes you for a spin, ooh lalala...' Ooh lalala indeed*, I thought, and wondered when Bill would make another announcement. I was sure there would be one.

The next week at rehearsals we all worked

really hard. I thought we sounded good, but that was only to be expected; Bill wouldn't have it any other way. And besides, Bill knew he could rely on us all to practise at home. That's what it's like in the cul de sac, we're all pretty reliable.

At the end of the evening Bill said, 'Well troops, stand smart, you're as good as you'll get and as I look at you all now, I can definitely say that we're ready for next week at Dean and Fraser. And, I can safely say, we'll do ourselves proud and raise a good amount for our chosen charity and enjoy ourselves at the same time. And that's not all, I'll tell you something else and it's this; having Poppy in the group, cul de sac member or not, has added something to our little group, on behalf of us all, Poppy, my dear, thank you.'

I must say I was slightly taken aback; not stunned of course, being stunned never seems to happen in the cul de sac, but I could see by some of the faces that other members were of the same mind as I was; Julie and Gladys in particular. I didn't want to cause trouble, not at this time of the year, peace and goodwill and all that. I went off with Beattie to make the tea.

'What do you think of Bill and his little speech?' Beattie said.

'I think what we all thought. Bill shouldn't single any one member out for praise. It isn't right, not when it's a cul de sac event, and especially when we've all put in so much time and effort to practise; and I'm including everyone in that, men and all. And I know we don't back-bite, and I'm sorry to even feel that I should say this, but if it was just Poppy singing it wouldn't have been the same as the group singing. Poppy just added to it, that's all. She's not the whole thing, nobody is.'

'I couldn't have said it better myself', Beattie said.

Bill appeared in the doorway. 'I thought this was the rehearsal for the Big Sing, not the big discussion,' he said.

It was no use. I know I should've bit my tongue, but I couldn't, goodness knows what Sid would've said, well, not much truth be told, but anyway I said it.

'Sarcasm doesn't become you Bill.'

Beattie gasped. As soon as I'd said it I wished the ground could've opened up and swallowed me.

'I didn't know I was being sarcastic,' Bill said. 'I was merely commenting on what I observed, two ladies, two friends, having a chat as they made the tea, no more no less. But I appear to have touched a raw nerve, and for that, ladies, I am sincerely sorry.'

'And I apologise for any raw nerves I may have touched,' I said.

'Ladies, I am not the one with the problem,' Bill said, and then he left the kitchen. A couple of minutes later we heard him say, 'The drinks will be with us in a tick, help yourselves to biscuits, please.'

The next week the singing at Dean and

Fraser went well. Over the few days that we sang we managed to raise one thousand and eighty-five pounds for our local 'Riding for the Disabled'.

'Job well done,' Bill said, and there were no extra thank yous for Poppy, either. I think we were all relieved about that.

The next event on the cul de sac calendar was the New Year Bash at Bill's. We cul de sac-ers were always informally invited at the end of the Big Sing. No such invitations had been issued this time, and it was less than two weeks to New Year's Eve. I wondered if I had actually put my foot in it good and proper. I thought of mentioning it to Sid, to get his reaction, and then I thought better of it. I 'phoned Beattie instead.

'Do you know if Bill's singled us out to be excluded from his New Year's Bash?' I asked.

'If you mean has everyone else been invited to Bill's and you haven't, then I can say you've nothing to worry about. As far as I know from speaking with Joan yesterday, and this is all I'm going on, no one has been invited, formally or informally.'

That was a relief to me at any rate. I would have hated to jeopardise any cul de sac event, so as you can guess, Beattie's news was a real fillip.

I heard a key in the door. Sid was coming back with the paper. I went and put the kettle on for the morning coffee. Sid really enjoyed his Americano in the morning; black with two spoonfuls of Manuka honey. It was that, he said, that kept him going.

When we sat down with the drinks Sid didn't automatically go to read his paper. I knew he was working himself up to something.

'Well?' I said.

'Well what?'

'What is it that you need to share?' (I'd recently been to a bonding class with Primrose at the Town Hall, and asking people to share seemed to be very relevant). It seems that asking people to share, encourages them to express themselves more fluently, at least that was what the instructor had said. So, I thought that it might be helpful in Sid's case.

'I've just seen something interesting. Poppy Sutcliffe's house is up for sale.'

'That is interesting,' I said.

'And there's something else.'

'There is?'

'Yes. I've bumped into Bill. He's invited us to the New Year Bash at his house. He said that this year's going to be a whopper', and then he winked at me.'

'He winked at you?'

'Yes.'

When I came off the 'phone to Beattie I was able to tell Sid the story, so far as I knew it.

'We're all invited. It's the same as every year, all the cul de sac's going to Bill's on New Year's Eve.'

'That's what I told you. I never thought it would be anything different,' Sid replied.

New Year's Eve came and we all went round to Bill's. Julie looked stunning in her new outfit, a frothy number with a blush pink bodice and lots of net in the skirt and as with most of Julie's outfits, a lot of sequins and seed pearls. Frank looked on admiringly.

Primrose and Brian were amongst the last to arrive. I don't know what Primrose had been feeding Brian over Christmas, but whatever it was, it had certainly put a spring in his step.

Everything was well under way when about an hour into the proceedings Bill stood up. 'There'll be another guest, a late arrival, due any time, I should think.'

'I thought we were all...' Sid nudged me,

'Let Bill finish, Rita.'

'What I want to say,' Bill continued, 'is that the next guest to arrive is someone you all know, but who isn't, at the moment, living in the cul de sac.'

'Poppy,' I said, before I realised it.

'Yes, it is Poppy,' Bill said. He carried on, 'Some of you may have noticed that her house was up for sale. Truth is, she's not been able to settle since the death of John, her husband. I've tried to help, tried to involve her in our events as much as possible, but it's no good. She's decided to move and live with her son. She's sold her house and will be moving in the New Year. I hope you'll make this last event of the season a happy one for her.'

Bill was interrupted in his speech by the ringing of the doorbell; twice in quick succession.

'I'd better get that,' he said, 'It'll be Poppy.'

ABOUT THE AUTHOR

Margaret Holbrook lives in Cheshire. She writes stories, plays and poetry and has had her work published in several anthologies.

In October 2012 she was a finalist in the Ovation Theatre Awards. Her short play *Soup for Starters* received an Honourable mention.

In June 2013 her one minute play, *Talk to me,* was a winner in the Gi60 play festival in Halifax.

Some of Margaret's work has been read on local radio.

Cul de Sac Tales is her second book.

Visit her website at www.margaretholbrookwrites.weebly.com